Novelettes and Short Stories of A. J. Cronin

A. J. CRONIN

Original publication dates:

"Lily of the Valley"
Hearst's International / Cosmopolitan magazine, February 1936

"Mascot for Uncle"
Good Housekeeping magazine, February 1938

"Child of Compassion"
Redbook magazine, June 1940

"The Portrait"
Hearst's International / Cosmopolitan magazine, December 1940

"The Man Who Couldn't Spend Money"
Redbook magazine, July–August 1946

"The One Chance"
Redbook magazine, March 1949

"The Innkeeper's Wife"
The American Weekly magazine, December 1958

Copyright © 1936, 1938, 1940, 1946, 1949, 1958 A. J. Cronin

ISBN: 978-1543220940

A. J. Cornell Publications

CONTENTS

NOVELETTES

Child of Compassion	4
The Man Who Couldn't Spend Money	51
The Innkeeper's Wife	98

SHORT STORIES

Lily of the Valley	130
Mascot for Uncle	159
The Portrait	185
The One Chance	214

CHILD OF COMPASSION

SHE WAS seated on the lawn under the copper beech playing very seriously with her children. She wore a white pinafore, rather crushed, and a ribbon that drew her brown hair straight back from her brow. Her legs were bare and ended in a pair of speckled sand-shoes. She was not yet seven, you see. And the children, of course, were her dolls.

As I came round the bend of the drive, I stopped to watch her while tenderly she shielded Sam's complexion—I felt sure it was Sam, the ugly one with the nose that had been glued on twice—with a tiny pink parasol. I couldn't help smiling—her gravity, her solicitude. And then, though my business was with Cook's lumbago and I had half a dozen calls before my evening surgery, I had to step between the beds of tall delphiniums to pass the time of day with her.

"Good afternoon, ma'am. And how, might I ask, is the family today?"

She looked up at me, a very little girl scenting that most distressing grown-up custom of "poking fun," and the sunlight fell into her big dark eyes. Then she smiled: a smile which flowed from her eyes, so slow and serious it bore a wistful quality until the dimples broke upon her cheeks.

"Master Sam," she said reflectively, "I must say, he's been a rather troubling boy. He doesn't *thrive.*" She considered Sam with pity and interest, as though even she had scarcely ceased to marvel at his constitution. "He's a nextrordinary delicate creature."

This, though sheer plagiarism from Nurse, was a good one. And the phrase was just: the dolls were a sad and battered crew. One had lost an arm, another an ear, a third the use of both her limbs; and Sam—Sam of the twice-glued-on nose—well, Sam!

Studying them, and her, I said:

"And where, ma'am, is the lovely new baby that a kind Tig gave you for Christmas? She had a beautiful dress that buttoned down the back. She had lace—real, most expensive lace—upon her petticoat; and she went to sleep when you laid her down."

She meditated whilst the sunshine slipped through the copper beech leaves and danced amongst her hair. Then she said:

"I'm so sorry, Tig. Charlotte wanted him. And anyway, I think I like my *inflicted* ones the best."

My lips twitched. But she said quickly:

"Please don't laugh. Truly I'm serious, Tig."

It was difficult. Her big round eyes were so solemn—solemn as the eyes of a little brown owl. Just as solemn as on that first day a year ago when I had been called to see her. She had measles. And I, newly qualified, very nervous and anxious to impress, must have made my examination a desperate affair—until, shattering my learned air, she had gravely declared: "You tickle so much I shall call you Tig."

Impossible not to laugh. And I laughed again now.

"You're a queer little thing, Susan."

"Am I?"

I fingered in my waistcoat pocket. The sweets called "clear gums" were in fashion then—hygienic, unimpeachable.

Susan advanced one small gritty palm, smiled her serious little smile.

"Thank you, Tig." She laid the sweet upon her lap and admired it, her head inclined to one side. "Yes, I do like ras'b'ry flavor," she reflected to herself.

A crunching on the gravel path disturbed us, and Charlotte came bounding over, followed by Nanny. She was like a little pony, was Charlotte, a healthy little pony, plump and firm, just a year older than her sister Susan; and she skipped up, her yellow ringlets tumbling about her round pink cheeks. Arrived, she gave a real actressy shudder and looked to me for approval.

"Our Susan's dolls! Aren't they horrid, nasty things?"

Our Susan flushed.

Charlotte let out a good-natured giggle and gave a

neat hop, skip and jump. Then her bright blue eyes spied the sweet on Susan's lap.

"O-oh," she shrieked, and laughing, pounced upon it, popped it into her own red mouth. Then she cried: "Can I have it, Susan? Can I really? You don't want it, or you'd have et it. And it's my birthday next week. Remember. The party—"

For a moment it looked as if Susan might have cried. But she didn't. She swallowed hard. Then she smiled her smile.

"Yes," she said, "the party."

Nanny made a sound with her lips, almost a snort, and waddled forward. Nice doings indeed, with sweets and whatnot! But what could you expect from an inexperienced young man, the ink not half-dry on his certificate. Shameful, it was! A competent woman, she'd been waiting the chance to put her foot down proper.

"Come now, Miss Susan. You'll get your death of cold on that damp grass." A severe side glance toward me. "Mrs. Williams been awaiting for the doctor this good half-hour, and suffering shocking, poor soul, she is. Come along now; it's time for bread-and-milk."

The last word had a hollow ring which spelt the ending of the day. But Susan made no protest. Rising to her feet, she gathered up her discreditable progeny and clasped them to her carefully. Charlotte pranced ahead with Nanny, singing a little tune, very gay. Susan trotted across the lawn behind them, alone. . . .

Of course, I went to the party. Everybody went to

Charlotte's party. It was a wonderful party, most wonderful: a party with a conjurer, and real rabbits, colored ice-cream—two sorts, strawberry and vanilla—the most glorious cake, with eight candles that really lit and melted beautifully, all over the shiny pink icing.

Harry Sinclayne, the father of Susan and Charlotte, was a widower; Ellen, his wife, had died at Susan's birth. He was a big man, red-faced and hearty, a stockbroker in Bristol. Impulsive, generous, prodigal of money and emotion, he kept his fine house in Clifton open to his friends. Friends? Why, in his own breezy way, he hadn't an enemy in the world! And as for his children? Well, Harry would have emptied his purse or stood upon his head for them all in one gay and boisterous breath. Charlotte, without doubt, was his favorite. Though he didn't know it and would have denied it angrily, deep down in his subconscious mind, he had never forgiven Susan the catastrophe of her birth. But Charlotte—ah, Charlotte was all right. "Like me, that kid," grinning genially. "Regular chip of the old block."

And now, on the flood of a bullish market, he had thumped the table—making Charlotte shriek—and decreed her party to be a paragon of parties. Or he would know the reason why! So stacks of little white chairs had arrived, and an important man, and heaps and heaps of lovely things. And Mrs. Williams, risen from her bed of sickness, and having words with the important man, had declared on her sacred soul she would soon be back again. But never mind, oh, never mind, it was on now—now!—the crackers snapping, the spoons chink-chinking on ice-cream saucers, everybody talking, laughing, nudging, eating, and the soapy scent of well-washed childhood rising warmly in the air.

In a corner, across a shivery mountain of blancmange, Susan was staring at Dicky. It was his first appearance. His people had come only recently to the town; and Dicky quite properly had come with them. He was eight and had all the attraction of a novelty. He had been dressed up in a blue sailor suit with a floppy bow, rather a nautical, stagy suit of the kind that adoring mothers love and children hate to wear. Yes, he distrusted the bell bottoms of his trousers sadly. There was, however, the compensation of a lanyard and a whistle. Dicky was proud of the whistle.

"It's terribly loud," he was assuring her. "There's a real pea in it. But Tally said I mustn't blow, cos it was rude. She has nerves. But I might let you try"—he paused cautiously—"after." Silence. Then he inquired: "Can you do long division?"

With grave wide eyes upon him, Susan shook her head from side to side.

"It's easy." He grinned upon her encouragingly and proceeded to further demonstration of his powers. "Look!" He pulled up one trouser-leg and rolled down his sock unblushingly. "I've got a hack on my shin. Awful, isn't it? It goes green and then yellow. It might even give me gangy-rene."

Susan did not blench. Instead her eyes grew round, her forehead creased with a divine compassion. Clearly she thought him a very nice little boy, and was prepared to discuss his morbidity intelligently. Just then, however, Charlotte bounced up with a train of little girls behind her. She was pink and laughing, excited, very important, everyone eager to be her friend. She paused, rather out of breath—she was really slightly the worse for trifle. Then she giggled.

"Our Susan has the awfulest dolls." They all laughed happily—all except Susan, who turned red, and Dicky, who stood doubtfully on the uncovered leg. "Really she has," nodded Charlotte brightly. "Yes, really. Ask her if you don't believe me. She likes them. Yes, really she does." All the little girls stared incredulously, and one on the edge of the group ventured another titter.

Susan looked as if she wanted to run away.

"It doesn't matter," said Charlotte kindly. "We're going to play Grand Old Duke of York." Rocking on one foot, she looked coquettishly at Dicky. "I choose you." But at that moment the door swung open, and Sinclayne burst into the room in his usual outrageous fashion.

"Where's my little Charlotte Russe?" he cried. "I haven't seen her for a whole long day." Unmindful of her dignity as hostess, he tickled her until she squealed, then hoisted her upon his shoulder.

"Don't, Father, don't! We're going to play Duke of York." She wriggled.

"Well—can't you play with me?"

"No, put me down," Father," she cried. "I didn't choose you. I chose Dicky."

CHARLOTTE AND Susan went away to school—not the little kindergarten at the foot of their own drive that only played at being a school—for they were growing up, thirteen and fourteen, oh, quite old now, as Susan said. No, they went to a real school, a first-class school, Sinclayne emphasized to me, as if to dull the pang the parting gave him. It was at Brighton. Healthy, he insisted, build Charlotte up, it would; as if that were necessary for Charlotte.

"Hanged if I know how to put up with myself without her," he muttered over our evening game of billiards. In melancholy style he chalked his cue. Markets were not so good of late. "House is like a graveyard without my Charlotte Russe."

I looked at him as he made the shot and missed.

"There's Susan too," I suggested. "You're missing her as well."

"Eh?" He raised his head, his face heavily congested from stooping, a bad, unhealthy color, I couldn't help thinking.

"There's a lot in Susan, you know. So quiet you'd never notice. But it's there."

He grunted.

"Susan's all right. Dumb little sprat. She's not—well, she doesn't *fill* the place like Charlotte." If he said that once, he said it twenty times within the passage of the long first term.

But there were holidays, of course; and Charlotte came back from time to time, grown extraordinarily in stature and composure, her ringlets restrained by a well-patted bow, her eyebrows inclined to spasms of critical elevation, but gladdening her father's heart for all that with talk of forms, prefects, and her marvelous skill in whacking a hockey-ball about.

Susan came too. And every time it was as though new luster had fallen on her. She didn't grow a lot; she still was very slight—in Mrs. Williams' words, but a small little bit of a thing. But the loveliness of her! It lay upon her like a bloom; sometimes it made me catch my breath.

Then came a staggering day. Only yesterday the battered dolls shoved away in an attic box. And now! Yes, it was staggering to find her home from school for good, her hair up, her skirts lengthened, her lisp finally departed, her warm, soft eyes twinkling with smiles at my bewildered look.

"Don't stare so, Tig, or I shall blush and start shedding hairpins." I laughed a little awkwardly, held by the misty beauty of those eyes, so deep and dark, smiling with such happy serenity.

"She blushes," broke in Charlotte with her bright laugh, "because she knows it becomes her." Beautifully frocked and blushing, our Susan tripped demurely downstairs.

"Ah, come now, Charlotte," Dicky put in quickly, "that's hardly cricket. Susan doesn't try—"

Dicky had dropped in, after his fashion, for a spot of tea—three good cups; that was a spot. Gone now was the sailor suit, the bow, the lanyard and the whistle—all vanished into the limbo of dreadful things to be forgotten. Gone, naturally, was that bruise; it had not fulfilled its awful foreboding of disaster. And Dicky was now a man of power and dignity, studying medicine at Bristol. Just like Dicky to have chosen to study at his provincial school. His people had money enough; he might quite easily have gone to Cambridge or to London. But Dicky had a certain solid bluntness in his nature which made him stand very consciously by his own especial gods. Lately I had kept an eye on Dicky, and I liked him. He was a strapping youngster who worked hard, played games admirably but not too much, and bore amongst his fellows a reputation for sound good sense. Those five swift years had placed me on the hospital staff, and I gave Dicky six months as junior dresser in my clinic. I didn't spare his work. But not once did he lose his temper or his keenness. That keenness ran throughout his character, a lively enthusiasm to succeed, to be thought well of, to justify himself. He had a marvelous confidence—a useful quality, but one which, in anyone less disarming than Dicky, might have perilously verged on self-sufficiency.

"And now that you're both home," I said, "and so ridiculously grown-up, what on earth is going to happen?"

Charlotte helped herself to cream and let her blue

eyes rest mockingly on Dicky.

"In the best romantic tradition," she announced, "I shall look out for a promising young man."

Dicky laughed sheepishly.

"And you, Susan?" I said. "It's a gloomy thought—but you'll do the same?"

"You forget, Tig," she answered, smiling, "I'm a new young woman. I don't sit down and wait until I'm asked. No, no. I'm going to have a career."

"And what sort of a career?"

"What's to prevent me from carrying a little black bag about like you?"

"You! Go in for medicine?"

"Why not? All the best new young women are self-supporting."

I stared at her. Though there were half a dozen women students in my own clinic, somehow I'd never thought of Susan in that light. I felt that she was only half serious.

But in the following month there came a turn of events which gave to Susan's answer a wholly grave significance.

ONE GRILLING August day they found Harry Sinclayne dead. He was in his office, seated at his desk in his shirtsleeves, his head fallen across a contract note upon the blotter. Syncope. I knew his heart to have been weak: a myocardial lesion. And I had warned him repeatedly, warnings which he had typically ignored. "You only live once, man, hang it all!

Well—why not?" I knew, too, that lately he had been worried in his affairs, that for months he had come home cursing the market, his luck, himself. . . .

It was a sad business, Harry's death, in more ways than one. For his papers were in serious disorder. He had bought heavily on a falling market. Changing his tactics, he had sold short recklessly and been caught by the turning tide. And he had been a spender. When the muddle was settled, Charlotte and Susan had each about eight hundred pounds, no more.

Six weeks after the funeral I had a talk with Susan. She had borne the shock of her father's death badly.

"I'm going in for medicine, after all," she said quietly. "I've quite decided. I'd like to be able to earn something. Charlotte wants to have a look round for a bit. She's going to friends at Brighton to rest. It suits her there. Then we'll take rooms, you see. Give up the house." She turned her head away, looking out at the lawn, pretending that she wasn't crying.

FIVE YEARS in the medical schools make less exacting demands upon temperament than might be fancied. There is a good deal of fun to leaven the grimness of the wards; moments when the phonograph is heard and cups of tea appear fortuitously in side rooms. And for the rest—human nature seen stark and unguarded evokes compassion more often than contempt. In those short years Susan learned more than the nomenclature of disease. She regained and did not lose her smile. Moreover, it was soon apparent how well suited were her qualities to the work. She had quiet, sure hands, a silent tongue and that secret sense of understanding more precious than fine gold. As the end of her studies drew near, I saw that she was going to be a real success.

And then one April forenoon I met Dicky in High Street. I stopped him.

"What d'you want here at this time of day?"

He put his hands in his pockets, looking happy, important.

"Came in to town to do some business."

"Business?"

"Yes—business." He looked happier, more important than ever. "Going to buy a ring."

"A ring?"—staring him up and down.

"Yes, of course." His boyish grin broke through at last. "For Susan!"

"Susan!" I must have gasped it.

"Certainly! Haven't you seen that we're hopelessly bowled over with each other? And have been for months."

No, I hadn't seen it. Perhaps I hadn't suspected Dicky of such penetration, such good sense. For there had always been Charlotte at his elbow, decorative, very elegant, quite obviously willing.

But anyway, there they were, Dicky and Susan, head over heels in love. And all her work and capabilities likely to go for nothing. A crying shame, I often told them. For of course they weren't going to wait. He had qualified in the previous autumn and was serving now a year's assistantship in one of the soundest practices in the country. It was in Wellgate, where life flows easily, pleasantly. And Dicky, at the end of his probation, would get his partnership—and then, Susan.

Every Sunday he drove from Wellgate to see her, in his new two-seater coupe. It was a high and rather bouncing car, which Charlotte named at sight the Hatbox, but it shone on those occasions like a battleship on flag-day. Dicky's face outshone the car. Moved from his complacency by Susan's beauty, he was an ardent lover. He would sound a little tune upon the horn outside her rooms: "Come out, my love, come out and play"; and she, racing downstairs, would fling open the door before the last note had faded on the quiet morning air. Usually they took the Hatbox to the country and picnicked in the open. They lay in the sun, ran races beneath the trees, made daisy chains, picked bunches of pink clover; they had mad discussions on this and that—how most politely to eat a ripe banana, and the many million miles a yellow butterfly might fly a day. They were quite absurdly happy. All that lovely summer they were the happiest pair on earth.

Easy enough for Dicky and Susan to forget that Charlotte existed! But Susan saw to it that they didn't forget. More often than not Charlotte was thrust by main force into the Hatbox. More often than not she munched sandwiches beside them, and lay beneath the trees, and joined in the sleepy arguments about butterflies and ripe bananas. Never for an instant was she made to feel herself unwanted, out of things. She wasn't given the slightest chance to sulk. Dicky continued to treat her with an easy comradeship: "We're great good pals, Charlotte. You and I. Aren't we, now?" And he would drop an acorn down her neck by way of emphasis.

So it went on until the autumn, when Susan came to take her final examination. Dicky expressed the bland desire that she would fail. "What earthly use," he teased her, "would it be if you passed, when you're going to marry me?"

But Susan smiled. She wasn't going to fail. Admitting his patronage, she had still the instinct to see her course completed—something ordered and achieved. She went up for the examination.

Her papers were excellent. This I knew at once, for at the previous election they had made me, quite unreasonably, an examiner in medicine. And her clinicals went well. She knew her work inside out; everyone liked her at the hospital. Before she went up to the wards for her final test in surgery, I was assured of her success.

IT WAS a Saturday; one of those quiet autumn days when the air is brittle with the hint of frost, when the trees stand very still—as though afraid the slightest movement will denude them of their sapless leaves. I was at home, my work at the hospital completed, my mind restless, strung somehow to a tension by the queer silence of the day.

Moving absently about the room, touching now this, now that, I suddenly looked up; and there, running up the drive, was Charlotte. Her haste seemed strange—Charlotte was always so poised, so sure of herself; then it seemed desperate. She raced through the open French window into the room, her face frantic with fear.

"Susan!" she cried. "Susan—" Panting for breath, she pressed her hand against her side; she couldn't speak another word.

I started forward.

"What's the matter? Charlotte, what's wrong?"

She began to sob hysterically.

"They telephoned," she gasped. "Telephoned from the hospital." And then she broke down completely, flung herself weeping upon the sofa. I could get nothing more out of her. But I saw, with a constriction of my heart, that something serious was wrong with Susan. I got the car in a hurry, drove to the hospital. In the vestibule I ran into the matron. For one whose composure was inveterate, she looked painfully upset.

"There's been an accident," she said quickly, "on the surgical side." And then she broke off, pressed her hands together. "She'll be all right, I think, I hope—but oh, it's horrible, horrible."

I stared at her with a set face. I knew that it was Susan.

"She was kneeling," the matron went on, and a

tiny shiver passed over her, "dressing an ankle—oh, I don't know what. One of the probationers slipped against the trolley. Carrying something, you see. An accident—oh, nothing but an accident. She stumbled and knocked over a reagent flask. It fell—it fell on Susan's face."

"Is she cut then, or hurt?"

The matron averted her eyes quite suddenly.

"It was acid," she stammered, "fuming nitric acid, that fell on her."

I felt myself go cold—quite cold. I couldn't see very clearly as I went up the stairs. Acid: nitric acid! A sudden wave of terror took me as I turned the door-handle and entered the small side room where Susan was. The room was darkened; but even in that darkness I saw enough. Susan was in bed, her face hidden completely by bandages. And she was passive, under the influence of morphia. Barclone, the senior surgeon, and Comyns, the eye man, were beside her. It was the sight of Comyns which paralyzed me with a sudden horror.

I advanced to the bed and stood beside them. For five minutes not a word was spoken; we simply stood there, the three of us, looking down at the bed. Then Barclone turned and took me by the arm to the door. Comyns followed. Outside I faced them, sick with dread.

"A shocking business," said Barclone at length. He fingered his watch-chain and would not look at me. "With a struggle we can save the sight. But the disfigurement—before God, I shrink from thinking of it. . . ."

The day came when the bandages were to be removed. I dreaded that day. I had seen the final dressings; I knew the full horror of it all. And Susan knew, too. That very morning she had asked for a mirror. There was no escape, no further pretext for delay—I gave it to her myself. For a full minute she looked at herself rigidly in the glass; then a long shudder ran through her body. The mirror slipped out of her hand; her head fell back wearily upon the pillow; she closed her eyes. All the morning she did not speak again.

About three o'clock Dicky and Charlotte appeared. They came into the room together: he with a spray of giant chrysanthemums, she with a home-made chocolate cake—a kind that Susan was especially fond of. They had an idea, perhaps, a vaguely optimistic idea of tea, a little party to celebrate the recovery. And they were smiling. For a second they stood in the doorway, a pair good to look upon, staring at Susan's face in that hard, uncurtained light. Then something went wrong with their smiles: they turned to shocked bewilderment and then to horror; it wasn't Susan that they saw, but another woman altogether. They hadn't expected this—oh, not this! Everyone had shrunk from telling them the savage truth. Perhaps some slight disfigurement, they had thought, perhaps a scar which might later yield to treatment.

EIGHTEEN MONTHS later Dicky married Charlotte. It was a quiet wedding—in Dicky's own words: "Naturally, we didn't want a beastly fuss." But they made up for the lack of fuss with a delightful honeymoon on the Italian lakes. And then they came back for the glorious business of beginning: the new partnership, the new house, and the new car—a real car this time, which put the Hatbox to shame. It was quite a thrilling time for Dicky and Charlotte.

Susan was content. Of course, Susan was content. Hadn't she wished it to be so? "Why should I waste his life?" It was the firm declaration of her resolution, not spoken aloud, but sounded by that secret voice in her own breast.

THERE HAD been a moment, I knew, a moment of weakness when her courage had faltered, and something within her reached blindly out to Dicky. Then, if he had still wished it, she would have flung herself, wounded face and more wounded soul, into the protection of his arms.

"Dicky—don't leave me, Dicky!"

But weeks had passed since that first rushing pity, and Dicky had waxed a little philosophical on his own account. There was sense in what Susan said, a heap of great good sense. Never was such a girl as Susan for solid common sense. That too was Charlotte's gushing tribute after the frightful afternoon when, confusedly, dreading to raise her eyes, she had come to Susan to blurt out the news:

"You see, Susan—Dicky, that's to say, Dicky and I—we want, we want to get married."

Susan had made it quite all right. All right? Of course it was all right. The best thing possible. Susan's present to the happy pair was quite magnificent. She came to the wedding. She shirked nothing of the stares and the whispered words:

"Isn't she marvelous, poor soul!"

"Such unselfishness."

"But, quite the right thing, of course." She was rather silent, it is true, but she smiled quite a bit—that stiff, twisted smile. Then she went straight back to the place in Wiltshire where she had found a billet.

She had her degree; but practice in the ordinary sense was now impossible for Susan. But she had found this post in an institution near Westplaine, a place of convalescence for the nervous states produced by overwork and worry. There her duties were mainly pathological; she was not called upon to mix with the cases; but she had at least some sort of work into which she threw herself passionately. I suspected that she was not happy in this work; it was all too isolated and inhuman amongst the test-tubes in that laboratory; but Susan never gave a sign. Old Mrs. Williams went often to see her, taking a cake or a pot of homemade preserve on the grounds that her child was being starved. And one evening on her return she said to me:

"To look at her—why, you'd think the whole bad business had never taken feather out of her." She sighed and shook her head. "But when you catch her unbeknown, there's a fearful sadness in them poor eyes of hers."

I gazed at her across my coffee cup.

"I wonder why she doesn't go more often," I speculated, "to see Dicky and Charlotte."

Lately, Susan's visits to Wellgate had become more and more infrequent.

"Indeed, sir, she'd want to go. But she's got the idea it's mighty unpleasant for them to have her. Bringin' back all that's gone before."

It was true. And it was a strange, sad reaction to Susan's generosity, that her reward should be merely the power to evoke unhappy memories.

For my own part, I was more often in Westplaine than in Wellgate. It was impossible not to like Dicky and Charlotte; there was no blame to them for what they had done; they swam cheerfully on a high tide of prosperity; there was a sly word, even, of "a certain coming event." The phrase was Charlotte's own—she wrote assiduously and had a pleasantly inconsequential touch with her pen. Oh, Charlotte was all right! But Susan—I never saw her nor thought upon her fortitude, but a lump rose up in my throat.

Late one winter afternoon I found myself unexpectedly at leisure, and so I motored down to Westplaine. It was dusk when I arrived. The lamplighter was going his rounds of the village—little points of light leaping out like torches in the darkness. I went into Susan's room and discovered her sitting in the fading light, a book upon her knee. Her small slight figure sunk in the window-seat. Missing her usual cheerful greeting, "Why, Tig, this is lovely!" I sang out:

"Stop reading at once. You can't see!"

She looked up quickly, and I was shocked to see that tears were streaming down her cheeks.

"I don't have to see," she answered in a low voice. "I know it. I know it almost by heart."

Silently I took the book out of her hand. She had lovely hands, small and white and well-kept—there was pathos in the care with which she tended them, as though in part they might atone for her disfigurement. I looked at the book. It was the "Essays of Elia." And it was open at the page: *Dream Children.*

"I've had an odd afternoon," she went on in a strained voice, and her eyes seemed to search a long way off. "It rained. I couldn't go out, and I started rummaging amongst my things. You'd never guess what I came across in that old trunk of mine." Her voice almost broke, but in a moment she went on meditatively, calmly: "Those battered old dolls I used to play with. I know I'm idiotically sentimental. But I can't help telling you. There they were, all of them. Wasn't it stupid? You remember Sam, the ugly one. You always said he was half-witted."

I could not speak, but stood suffused by the memory of that scene upon the lawn: the sunlight pouring down upon a little girl, touching her eager face, her lovely hair. There she had sat, waiting, waiting eagerly on life, with the sunlight in her eyes. . . .

"Oh, Susan," I cried at last. "Is there nothing, nothing that can be done to make you happy?"

There was a long pause; then she said:

"I don't know. Oh, I don't know. But I feel—I feel some day there might be perhaps—some day."

HOW FAST the years came piling one upon another!

Five years Susan had been at her research in Westplaine—she was almost twenty-nine.

At Wellgate the senior partner had retired; the practice was now Dicky's, and he worked it with a young assistant. Charlotte and he had moved to a better house, where they entertained largely—just the right people. Two fine boys now raced and tumbled about the grounds. They hardly knew of their Aunt Susan; they never spoke of her.

And then one day Susan came unexpectedly to see me. She sat down, and stripping off her gloves, she looked across at me steadily, yet nervously.

"I'm going to be married."

"What!" I almost jumped from my chair. And then, at the sudden color flooding her brow, I realized how much my crude amazement must have hurt her. I tried clumsily to cover my confusion. "Sorry, Susan. But you really did take my breath away! Tell me all about it."

"His name is David Learworth," she answered, in that same steady voice. "He has been at Westplaine for three months. Resting, you understand. He'd been overworking."

"More, Susan." I said, impatiently. "Tell me more about him."

"Don't be alarmed, Tig." The hint of a smile—that old quiet smile—played about her lips. "I can almost see you jumping to the wrong conclusion. But there isn't anything wrong. David is straight as a die. He's a doctor. For the last ten years he's been running the hospital at Milburn."

"The hospital at Milburn!" And then I remembered. "David Learworth. I know! Of course, I know. He's a coming man. His monograph on amnesia made quite a sensation a year ago. Why, he's quite brilliant."

"He's quite wonderful." Her voice was low, colored by a new happiness; her whole body seemed irradiated by happiness. "He is the last man who might have been expected to love a woman like me. He is brilliant, handsome, sensitive, kind. Oh, he has real nobility. And he has gone behind this hideous face of mine and found my soul. Think of it! You can't believe it—I can scarcely believe it myself. But it's true. Don't think I've jumped at this happiness. It's all come gradually. And I've done everything to kill it. I've tried a hundred times to put David off. Just as I did with Dicky. But David isn't like Dicky. I'm not running Dicky down; I don't blame him. But I'm glad"—her eyes shone—"oh, I'm glad almost that things happened as they did, now that I've found

David. He won't be put off. He won't, I tell you. Because he knows that all this ugliness isn't *me*. He loves the real me. He's going—he's going to marry me." Her voice broke: her face was bathed in quivering brightness. Somehow, I couldn't look at her. It was so incredible! I wanted to rise with answering delight; I couldn't. All the long afternoon which we spent together, I kept feeling myself unconvinced, strangely confused.

THE FOLLOWING Sunday, as we had arranged, I went to Westplaine to see David Learworth. Despite Susan's eulogy, or perhaps because of it, I had a queer distrust of Learworth.

I found him charming—completely charming. He was young, not more than thirty-four, with a tall, spare figure, a thin face, dark, flashing eyes and nervous sensitive hands. No wonder that Susan glowed as she saw him gradually win me around. We had a long walk, the three of us, and then an intimate tea in Susan's rooms. I studied him carefully. And it was true—it was as she had said. He loved Susan; his eyes followed her about, lingering upon her with a dark tenderness.

Before I came away, he was alone with me for just two minutes. And turning, he said, with almost fierce sincerity:

"Now do you believe? Don't think I haven't seen you watching me the whole afternoon. I do love her. From the first instant I saw her, I was drawn to her—

yes, compelled to her. She is like no other woman. Beauty—what is it? It's a standard which any man may vary! It changes in every latitude. But my feeling for Susan won't change. It is above change."

His queer and restless vehemence almost startled me. But how could I find fault with him for loving Susan with such feeling! The light shining in her eyes was warrant for any vehemence. I pictured the slow dawning of that light—the first meeting with David, the first incredulous recognition of his interest, the gradual breaking down of her reserve, the doubts and fears and agonies of disbelief, and finally the dazzling knowledge that she was at last beloved. I went home thoughtfully, a trifle dubiously, convincing myself a miracle had happened.

Then one week later I had a telegram from Dicky: *"Coming to see you this afternoon. Important."* And Dicky arrived in haste two hours after his wire. He had altered a little by success: stouter, a little thin upon the crown, perhaps a trifle self-important. And without preliminaries, he flung himself into an easy chair, lit a cigarette from his monogrammed gold case, and exclaimed curtly:

"I saw Susan yesterday! Went specially down to Westplaine. Missed a whacking important case to do it." A certain irritability lay behind his words. He took a quick puff at his cigarette, threw me a determined glance. "You've heard about this affair—her affair with this Learworth fellow."

I didn't like his tone.

"Affair? Surely more than an affair, Dicky. You mean her marriage."

He made an impatient movement with his hand, flicked his ash into the fireplace.

"Marriage be hanged! The thing is absurd. Absolutely absurd. I've got a certain feeling of responsibility toward Susan. And I'm going to stop it. You've got to help me. I've asked her to be here this afternoon. We've got to thresh the whole thing out and finish it."

"Finish it," I echoed. "My dear Dicky—surely you exaggerate that responsibility you speak of. Even if we don't exactly approve of what she's doing, Susan is her own mistress. She can do exactly as she pleases."

"She doesn't understand," he interrupted. "Her feeling toward Learworth is making her quite blind. But I'm not blind. And I've been making inquiries. I don't trust the fellow an inch."

I stared at him, knowing that he had placed a finger upon the very heart of my doubt. Perhaps that was why I suddenly felt irritated.

"For heaven's sake, don't call him 'the fellow,' Dicky. He's better qualified than you. And a coming man. He's made Milburn one of the most up-to-date mental hospitals in the country."

"Mental hospital!" he threw back derisively. "Why don't you say asylum, if you're out for plain speaking?"

Indignantly I made to answer, but at that moment the door opened and Susan walked into the room. I broke off; Dicky rose hurriedly. Yet there fell a very awkward pause; she saw that we had been discussing her, and it seemed to send a wincing shadow across her face. But she said quietly:

"Here I am, then, Dicky. I had your wire. It's all very important and mysterious. But I can't stay long. So go on with what you were saying."

DICKY GOT rather red about the gills. He studied the glowing end of his cigarette. And then with sudden determination he declared:

"I will go on. I've got to go on. It isn't exactly pleasant, but it's got to be done. This—this business of your marriage, that's what I'm here to talk about."

She answered slowly: "But we had all this out at Westplaine."

"Not out enough, Susan," he replied doggedly; "not nearly enough. You must be wise. Really you can't go through with it."

She stared at him incredulously; then a wave of nervous color rose betrayingly to her brow.

"You of all people, to talk like that! Because you didn't marry me, I'm to be denied happiness all my life! You must be mad to talk like that."

He paused, then said deliberately:

"It isn't I—that's mad."

The words struck like a thunderbolt into the room.

She gasped: "What—what exactly do you mean?"

He looked her straight in the face. "Learworth. That's who I mean. He's not normal. The moment I saw him, I felt he was unbalanced. And now I know. I'm positively convinced of it."

There came another dreadful pause; then, before she could collect herself to answer, he went on:

"Learworth never had a breakdown. It was something more than that, or I'm very far mistaken. Something not far off mania. I went out to Milburn specially. They wouldn't tell me much. How could they tell me—the fellow acting as his deputy there looked scared, the instant I raised the question. There's something queer behind it. But I've put two and two together. You know how a man can go when he spends all his days cooped up working in an asylum. He's liable to go queer. That's how Learworth's gone. And more!" His voice rose a little, more dogged than ever. "I made further inquiry. There's a mental tendency in his family."

Susan had paled to the lips. Her body stiffened; she uttered a little choking cry.

"So that's it!" she whispered. "You—you make him out to be mad, because—because he wants to marry me."

"No, Susan! No!" He leaned forward, in a shamefaced yet determined way. "You can't, you mustn't say a thing like that. It's horribly unfair."

"It's you who are horribly unfair. To me, and to David as well. I know all about his illness. And you're wrong, horribly wrong. He's very highly strung. He was overworking; he had a breakdown; it was a case of nerves, nothing more. How dare you mention such a word as you have done! Can't you, oh, can't you understand? Oh, how can you hurt me like this? It's cruel. It's inhuman."

Dicky averted his head in silence. Then Susan, who had been crying softly, controlled herself, stood up.

"I love David," she declared in a low, firm voice. "I love him with all my heart. I'm going to marry him. Nothing will make me give him up. *Nothing!*" Turning, she went out of the room.

THAT SUMMER the marriage took place. I was worried. I didn't know what to do about it. And what could I do? I visited Milburn myself: I made every investigation. Learworth had once been taken with a nasty nervous breakdown, it was admitted. But many a man has had that in his time. As for his family history, it was a fact that his uncle had committed suicide. A stolid country jury had added the inevitable rider: *whilst of unsound mind.* But that did not damn Learworth. Nothing might be in it. Certainly there was nothing in Learworth's conduct to confirm Dicky's suspicion, absolutely nothing. He was in every way admirable, perfect. Yet here, irrationally, lay the source of my uneasiness:

Learworth was too good to be true!

Yet Susan found him true enough. They had gone to Llynfan, a tiny fishing village set remotely on the north Wales coast. There they had taken a house, for they had planned—and how Susan loved that planning!—a whole year's holiday. A long time! But it was well deserved. Neither had taken a holiday for years; they had their happiness; they meant now to hold it in this faraway place at the foot of the mountains and the edge of the sea.

And how closely they held it! Susan wrote regularly—letters which were a joy to read, and to read again for the sheer delight of knowing she was happy. They breathed of happiness, these letters, each word enriched with the glory of the mountains, the deep tranquility of the sea, the mystical beauty of a soul. They brought visions of long, still evenings, and Susan sitting by the open window, while fans of light went dancing across the waters, and a tang of woodsmoke hung upon the air; visions of the warm darkness of the night closing down upon her as with a sigh, a breath of happiness.

I felt a keener zest in life; my anxiety disappeared; I looked forward to the treat of visiting Llynfan in spring.

And then, suddenly, quite suddenly, the tone of Susan's letters altered. I noticed it instantly in the letter which came upon the last day of October. It was her usual bulletin, filled with a cheerful account of all that had been done and all that was to do. But the key was different. Beneath the words there ran an undercurrent of concealment.

The succeeding letters were the same, or rather they grew worse. They came as regularly as before; but they were strained and artificial. Then for an en-tire fortnight nothing came. Finally on the twenty-first day of December a note arrived which really startled me. Two lines written in a hurry upon a half-sheet of notepaper: *"Can you please come down? I need you. At once."*

NEXT DAY I arrived in Llynfan. It was a gray afternoon. The clouds hung low upon the mountain, and a squally wind buffeted the rain hard into my face as I headed down the single village street. Susan had not met me at the station—this in itself oppressed me—but I had little difficulty in finding the house. It was the old coastguard station, a white stone dwelling, flat-roofed and square, set solidly against the gale upon a cemented court. A flat pole rose starkly from one corner; some withered fuchsias flanked the path. How gay it must have been in sunshine, with a strip of bunting on the staff and the fuchsias burning against the brilliant whiteness of the walls! But now there was no sun—only mist and rain—rain and that lashing wind upon the sea.

There was no need to knock. Susan had been watching from the window, and she ran to meet me at the door. Her fingers were trembling as we shook hands.

"I'm sorry I couldn't meet you." Her lips were trembling too. "I've been with David. But he's gone out now. Rather unexpectedly, you see."

She was glad I had come; every gesture expressed relief—but in all her movements there was a queer nervousness. She was on edge. I could have sworn that her eyes were red with weeping. She had on a dark brown dress which gave, it seemed, a curious new dignity to her slight figure. Holding my arm, she took me into the living-room and sat down beside me on the sofa before the fire. Even then she did not release her clasp upon my sleeve. It worried me.

I put aside her offer of food—I had lunched on the train—and slipped my arm across her shoulders.

"Here I am, then, Susan. Tell me."

SHE AVERTED her head; I felt her suddenly go limp. For a time she did not speak; then in a low voice she said:

"I've really got to tell you. Oh, I must tell someone. I've tried to keep it to myself, because I thought it was disloyal to speak. But I can't—oh, I can't keep it any longer." And she dropped her head upon my arm and burst into tears. A full two minutes passed before she could compose herself. Then, staring straight in front of her, she faltered: "It was so wonderful in the beginning. That's what makes it so terrible now. David—oh, I cannot tell you how wonderful he was. He was everything I'd wanted, everything I'd longed for. We were the whole world to each other."

"I know. I saw that from your letters."

"And then the awful thing happened. Quite suddenly." She closed her eyes as if at a sight she could not endure. "We were at dinner one night. And David—he had been quiet all day, very quiet and strange—he suddenly gripped his knife and pointed it at me. 'Stop watching me,' he said; 'I've been spied on quite enough lately.' I thought at first he was trying to make fun. I laughed and said: 'Don't be silly.' But he stared across at me—and oh, the look in his eyes, it frightened me. And he said: 'My God, I believe you're linked up with those devils who are watching me.' Oh, it was frightful—the shock, that look on his face—worse, far worse than his words." She hesitated; then biting her lip, she forced herself on. "It wasn't a joke, after all. I was all taken aback. And I was frightened, terribly frightened. I asked him to explain. I came over and tried to take his hand. But he shoved me away, jumped up and went shouting and banging out of the house." She broke down again, completely, let her head fall against my shoulder. "What's the use," she cried helplessly, "what's the use of trying to tell you? That was just the start. That night when he came in, he locked the door. He didn't speak to me for days. And now that he does speak—oh, it's such nonsense! You'll see for yourself. It's gone on from bad to worse. I've struggled and hoped and prayed all these weeks. But nothing does any good. David is—oh, he's not the David that loved me! He is queer. He is"—she sobbed out the words—"he really is out of his mind."

A bar of silence fell, broken by a sudden gust of wind and rain upon the windowpane. Then a quiet tapping of the fuchsia branches began, *tap-tap, tap-tap,* coming and going, coming and going interminably.

What on earth was I to say?

And then the outer door swung open, there came the stamp of noisy footsteps on the stone hall, and David flung into the room. One glance was enough. He had altered beyond recognition, his eyes wild, his cheeks gaunt, his wind-blown hair all tangled upon his brow—his whole expression stealthy, glittering. And now he stood with the rain dripping from him, his feet planted wide apart upon the flags, staring at us as we sat together.

"Very touching!" he cried at last; and a sneer curled his lip. "But what the devil are *you* doing here? I haven't asked you. And I'm the reason of all asking. I, David Learworth, am the reason of all asking and all being."

Susan rose at once and went to him, her manner indicating all too painfully how often she had tried to pacify him in the past.

But he thrust her aside and declared excitedly:

"I say that I am the reason, omnipotent and universal. But no one will believe me. They're all against me. Every hand of every man. All unreason, all unbeing, all around me. They've drawn a cordon round this house. But I'll get the better of them yet—you'll see—you'll see!" His eyes dilated; he waved his arms and gave a short, wild laugh. Then he spun round and marched out of the room.

Dead silence. Susan turned away, hiding her face, and drew the curtains. She was a long time at the window. Then, without looking at me, she said:

"You see—it's no use evading things any longer. You must make him promise to go away—to go away for treatment. I've asked him a dozen times. But he won't agree. You must make him go." A note of fierce intensity crept into her voice. "He'll be cured. He must be cured. He'll be back again just—just as he was before."

I lowered my eyes: her hope struck me as both pitiful and forlorn. But I said:

"I'll do my best, Susan."

There was another silence; then she asked:

"Would you like to go upstairs now?"

OUR SIMPLE meal was cooked by Susan herself—the maids had left abruptly on account of Learworth's strange behavior. And now, though she fought for cheerfulness, she looked worn out, piteous.

Suddenly Learworth threw down his spoon with a clatter. He lay back in his chair: he had insisted on wearing a purple dressing-gown.

"I can't swallow that soup," he declared loudly. "It is not fit soup for me. I deserve food worthy of a king."

"It's very good soup," I said sharply, "and you ought to be grateful to Susan for making it."

He looked at me sullenly, then began to throw quick darting glances about the room. There was real malevolence in his face. It frightened me for Susan's safety. I was glad, doubly glad, that I had come.

He remained lolling back in his chair until she

served the next course: a dish of mutton cutlets carefully browned.

"You'll have some of this, David," she ventured almost timidly. "Please."

He snatched the plate without a word and began to eat voraciously. Then in a moment he started off again, riding his delusion, working himself about restlessly as he spoke:

"There's a cordon drawn round the house. Under cover of the darkness, you understand. That is the lot of the mighty, the penalty of high omniscience. But I'm not afraid. And I'm not defeated." He laughed harshly, with a sort of sly merriment. "No, no. That is beyond the power of man. To defeat the undefeatable. I have a way to escape. A glorious way to escape."

I DREW in my breath. It was sheer mania. And so I said, as reasonably as I could:

"There are no spies around this house, David. You are sitting here eating your dinner quietly with your wife and me."

He raised his eyes sharply; then he lay back and began to laugh again. He roared with laughter; suddenly he shut it off as though he closed a trap.

"My wife!" he cried. "I haven't got a wife. I'm finished with her. She's in league with them—my enemies."

The feverish note in his words was terrifying, the look upon his face a maniac's look. I jumped up and faced him; for Susan's safety and his own, I saw that he must be restrained immediately.

"Come, David," I said soothingly, "there's a good chap. It's no use upsetting yourself like this." And I made to take his arm.

But frenzy was in him now: the pent-up frenzy of long, brooding weeks. He struck me violently on the jaw, threw back his head and loosed a wild, animal cry.

As I fell across the table, Susan flung herself in a panic at his feet.

"David, David!" And she clasped her arms round his knees.

But he kicked himself free. Before I could rise, he dashed to the door and wrenched it open.

"I'll show them now," he shouted. "I'll show you all this instant. It's my power. Out and away! Like Ariel! Omnipotent and free!"

Susan screamed; but he was gone. I rushed after him frantically, my head still swimming, calling on him in the name of God to stop. He was before me on the stairs, racing madly upward. I heard his breath come back, a high, dissevered panting, through the darkness. I didn't know what he was going to do. I tried all I could to overtake him. Fear ran coldly through my veins. Then, on the top landing, he burst through an opening which gave upon the roof to a wooden platform used for signaling to ships at sea. Quick as a cat he clambered through into the outer darkness. There, for an instant, I saw his figure outlined—monstrous and dark, towering with a maniacal resolution. Shuddering, I saw him raise his arms, god-like, invoking some unseen power. Behind me I heard Susan's voice choking upon the cry:

"David! *David,* come back!"

Then as I struggled to gain the roof, he shouted in that demented voice:

"Like Ariel! With wings like Ariel!" And with arms outstretched as if he had the power of flight, he hurled himself forward, plunging out and downward from my sight.

Through the lost moaning of the wind and the booming of the surf beyond, through the agony of Susan's shriek, I heard the crash of his body as it struck the concrete court below. Then Susan fainted—fell limply into my arms. . . .

SPRING CAME. The lilacs burst into blossom, and from the flowering chestnut trees little white petals drifted lazily like wings. The earth sang with a myriad of tiny voices.

In Wellgate the rooks circled high, cawing about their nests; the air was calm—so calm the chiming bells merely rippled upon the surface of the stillness. And Susan was in Wellgate with Dicky and Charlotte, all the coldness and misunderstanding of the last two years wiped out by her necessity. They had taken her at once, unhesitatingly.

I went often to see her, for I was still afraid; I felt on me a heavy shadow of reproach. Not that I blamed myself for David's death. He at least was better off, soaring that wide oblivion with Ariel, than shut up miserably in a padded cell.

But Susan?

I said one day to Dicky: "Does Susan—does she really—"

He gave me a searching look, and paused: we were strolling in the garden together after dinner: then, inspecting the glowing end of his cigar, he said in the same odd fashion:

"She goes out into the country a lot. Walking by herself. You know that?"

I did not follow his train of thought.

"And why not? It's good for her to get about."

"You know where she goes, of course?"

His manner arrested me. I shook my head, looked at him inquiringly.

"She goes to Barcraig," he said slowly. "To that house they're converting under the county scheme. Yes, that's where she goes, and potters about. Quite quietly, you understand. She doesn't mope. She's not hysterical. It just seems to give her a funny sort of comfort. Out at the old house at Barcraig."

Now, indeed, I knew that Susan knew. Barcraig was five miles from Wellgate, a tiny, lovely village, nested in rolling pastureland where clover fields abounded and honeysuckle drooped across the hedgerows. But no mere love of quietness had taken Susan to this spot. Oh, the motive could be felt, but not explained; for in Barcraig, they were making a home for children mentally deficient.

EARLY IN the previous year I had been invited to join the congress at Toronto in connection with the centenary of the Society of Medicine. I had accepted. And as arrangements stood, my departure fell due about the end of June.

The days drew on; the evenings lengthened; the time of my sailing for Canada was at hand. On the eve of my departure we were alone, Susan and I, seated in the library at the hour of dusk. I hadn't switched on the lights; I knew that Susan loved the concealment of the lingering twilight. A long silence had fallen between us. Then she said:

"Don't look so absurdly sad, Tig." She was actually smiling at me. "I know you don't want to go. But I want you to. You'll be better out of the way. And three months isn't long. You'll come back."

I started. If I could not read her mind, she could most uncannily read mine.

"Certainly I'll come back." Surely that wasn't all I could find to say! "And you'll be all right, Susan. Of course you will."

"Of course."

"Dicky is very good."

"Yes, he is very good."

Silence came again. The fading light fell slanting through the window upon her full figure, and gave her a strange, symbolic dignity. All the inner beauty of her soul seemed to flow out around her. Transfigured, she became majestic, noble, a figure of courage that would not know defeat. Suddenly she looked at me steadily and said:

"You have been very good to me, Tig. And I want you to know that I'm not afraid. I know what I've got to face. I've faced it all along. And if it should be the worst, there may be consolation for me, after all."

"You are very brave, Susan." I could hardly find my voice. "Very brave. More than anything—I want you to be happy."

There was a long pause. Finally she murmured:

"Don't you remember you said that once before? Ages ago, it seems. But you said it. And I told you that I had faith, that I believed something was coming to me"—her voice fell till it was almost inaudible—"something that would wipe out all the pain and all the sorrow. Forever."

I hardly dared to put the question.

"And do you still believe that, Susan?"

She nodded her head slowly; and into her scarred face there flowed a sweetness that was profound. She said distinctly:

"Yes, I do believe. And I'll hold on to it all I can."

The next day I sailed for Canada.

I had arranged with Dicky that he should send a cable the moment he had news for me. And through the opening days of the conference, while my mind was occupied by the procedure of the Council, something within me stood apart, waiting—waiting for the arrival of that vital, flimsy slip.

Two weeks slipped past and no cable had come. Another week, and there was still no news. Then one morning, at the end of July, I had word of Susan. Not the cable I had expected but, quite undramatically, a letter, a long and detailed letter from Dicky. Swallows were wheeling outside my bedroom window, and the poplars opposite stood straight like sentinels, as I opened the stiff gray envelope. I noticed that my hands were shaking as I drew out the closely written sheet. And then, in a moment, I knew it all.

Susan was all right—my heart turned over with an exquisite relief! But her baby was dead; it had been stillborn.

I gave a long sigh.

THE CONFERENCE dragged on. I had to make a tour with a subcommittee of delegates—Quebec, Montreal, Winnipeg, Vancouver; but my heart wasn't in the work. I had no further news from England. Nor did I wish it. In my heart there was a vague dread. Yes, now I dreaded to know the sequel of this last calamity.

And then, in the middle of September, I sailed for home. I reached Southampton on the twenty-first day of that month. Now, with the perversity which governs our emotions, I felt upon me the need of haste. The train was not quick enough. I hired a car and drove direct to Wellgate.

It was a shining day, one of those clear September days when the air holds the warmth of summer, and the land the glorious coloring of autumn. The orchards were in full bearing, the fields yellow with the stubble. A sheen lay upon the earth.

The car gave out a note like the humming of a homing bee. And I felt that I was home as we ran into Wellgate and came up the drive of Dicky's home. But my heart was thumping as I rang the bell and went into the familiar house. Charlotte and he were in the library. Taken by surprise, they stared, then jumped up; they fell upon me, overwhelmed me with their welcome. Yet through it all I felt that heavy anxious beating in my breast.

"And now," I said, "where is Susan?"

The two exchanged a look, a baffling look which confused and startled me.

"You haven't heard?" Charlotte asked.

"You've written nothing," I said quickly. "I haven't had a letter for weeks."

"You didn't write yourself," put in Dicky. "Not a word."

I stared at him in sudden anxiety.

"For heaven's sake," I cried, "what's all this evasion about? Tell me the worst. Where is Susan?"

His face revealed nothing, but he said one word:
"Barcraig."

Was he mocking me? Was he afraid to speak?

"It's no use telling you," he said in the same slow voice. "Go out to Barcraig."

They were both looking at me, Charlotte and he, with that curious, intent regard. I couldn't stand it.

With an exclamation I swung round and shot out of the room. I gave the man an order, jumped into the waiting car. As we ran through the narrowing lanes, I sat hunched in the seat, torn by a fierce anxiety. Why was Susan in Barcraig, where she had made those sad and solitary pilgrimages? In Barcraig, where broodingly she had gone, filled by the precognition of disaster? I was afraid.

At the gates of an old house I stopped the car and got out. Though I had often passed nearby, I had never been to the place before, and now, expecting the worst, I approached the lodge. It was a pretty cottage covered with red creeper; the gates were open; the drive stretched out in a long, trim curve, bordered by beds of double chrysanthemums. Nervously, I rang the bell. Immediately the porter appeared. He was a young man; and he was smiling. Hardly knowing how I put the question, I asked for Susan.

"Yes sir," he said at once. "I've just come down from the house. And the Doctor is on the front there now. She's been busy all morning." And he added, communicatively, and rather importantly: "We had the committee out for lunch."

I STARED at him; then a light broke upon me—quite dazzling. I cried:

"Then—she's in charge here!"

His face expressed genuine surprise.

"Why, yes sir. Dr. Sinclayne's the medical officer here. We'd ought to have a lady doctor, the children being so young."

I did not wait to hear another word. Turning, I made off along the drive. I felt a queer excitement, and a queer nostalgia: the memory of another day, of another drive where I had walked a long, long time ago. I hurried on. The peace, the seclusion of the place, was indescribable; the stillness sang with a note of happiness; the air was full of the aroma of the chrysanthemums.

I passed a field which had been the paddock; there rabbits sat sunning themselves. I heard laughter, the sound of children's laughter. Then the house swung into view, its mellowed front rising from the shaven lawn.

And then I paused, overcome by what I saw. Upon the lawn was Susan, her small, slight figure limned against the trees. And around her was clustered a band of small children. Noisily and unafraid, they played about her. Their laughter rose in happy waves. Two children held her by the hand. Their faces were uncouth and dull—but they clung to her without fear. One little boy no more than four was clutching at her skirts. His small, vacant eyes, stamped by the weakness of his kind, gazed up at her with love. He rubbed his little misformed brow against her knee. A terrible emotion of joy and awe rose up and caught me by the throat. Tears rose burning to my eyes. It was the look that dwelt upon her.

There, upon the lawn, in dignity and gentleness she stood. The sun fell full upon her, and in her ravaged face there was tenderness and peace.

THE MAN WHO COULDN'T SPEND MONEY

I HAVE known Joe Mardent most of my life—our boyhood friendship began, more than thirty years ago, in the North Country town of Shalehaven. Joe was an only child who had lost his parents in the Tynecastle Fair disaster of 1900, when a wooden grandstand collapsed at the County Show, killing over one hundred persons. Thus, at the age of eight, Joe became a charge upon his aunt, a middle-aged woman in poor circumstances, with five children of her own and a shiftless husband who worked intermittently as a ship's fitter in the Tynecastle yards. Although Sarah Mardent's nature was not unsympathetic, the endless struggle to make ends meet had soured and hardened her—she drudged along, always in dread of the poorhouse. In such a household Joe could not be truly welcome. From the moment he entered it, his easy childhood was at an end.

Do not imagine that Joe was ill-treated or starved—Aunt Sarah was no tyrant, and there was usually a dish of pease meal in the cupboard to stave off the more urgent pangs of hunger. But he had to work hard for his keep. In the mornings he rose at five to "go out with the cans"—that is, to do a milk round. After school he delivered newspapers. At weekends he ran errands for Harpole, the local grocer. And in the holidays he was sent to help with the harvest, to cut hedges, to do any of a dozen and one jobs which might bring in a few pence to this eternally needy household.

It was not the labour which affected Joe, for he was a wiry little chap, but this everlasting sense of being on the verge of destitution bit into his soul. He was a sensitive boy, and where another might have grown sharp and callous, Joe suffered acutely, less perhaps from his actual privations than from the humiliations, both physical and spiritual, which these forced upon him. He never had a coin in his pocket, like the other boys, to spend on sweets or marbles. Whenever he asked his Aunt Sarah for a penny for any of the treats, such as the visiting bioscope, which occasionally enlivened our community, he received always the same reply.

"I'm sorry, Joe," his aunt would sigh. "We simply can't afford it."

We boys never paused to analyze Joe's sensations when he could not come with us, but darted away with an indifferent laugh, leaving him alone, staring after us. Yet we all liked him, and respected his capacity for enduring his woes in silence. Only once, when he was about fifteen, and on the point of leaving school, did he reveal himself to me. Agnes Harpole, a girl in our class, was giving a "social" to mark our "breaking-up," and Joe had accepted an invitation on the strength of a long-standing promise of his aunt to give him a new suit. On the evening of the entertainment I called for Joe. He was waiting by the lamp-post at the street corner, in his ragged everyday clothes: a torn blue jersey. old made-down trousers and cast-off boots.

"Why aren't you changed, Joe?"

"No suit. I'm not coming."

It was dusk, but the overhead gas caught his pale strained face, shaded by a cloud of chestnut hair. In a pained, determined voice, he brooded:

"I've had enough of this. I'm going to get on, make money—if it kills me."

THERE WAS little opportunity in the Shalehaven district for poor boys, even the clever ones like Joe. Coal-mining and shipbuilding were our twin industries. If a lad came from a family of miners he usually "went underground"; if not, he was absorbed by one of the yards on the Tyne estuary, some twenty miles away. And so, while my father, who was the local doctor, managed to scrape together the fees to start me upon my medical studies at the Armstrong College, Joe entered the "yard" as an apprentice. Because of his slight physique, perhaps also because his uncle was widely known as a bad worker, he could not find a place with one of the large companies, but was forced to check in at Grigson's, a small private firm on the Shalehaven side, with a personnel of about five hundred men, engaged mainly in the construction of paddle steamers, tramp cargo boats, and an occasional vessel for the Argentine frozen-meat trade.

It was stiff work for a youngster of sixteen, and the long day was increased by the tedious journey to and from Shalehaven by workmen's train. In spite of this, Joe voluntarily enrolled in the Tynecastle night-school, and attended classes there four evenings in the week. These classes were free; otherwise, Joe could not have taken them, since he was surrendering his wages to his aunt, except for the small sum essential for his daily transportation. His midday lunch "piece" he brought from home. He could not afford cigarettes like the other apprentices, and for the same reason he never tasted beer, took out girls, or patronized the theater.

AFTER ABOUT two years of this uneventful existence, a peculiar accident befell Joe. Whether he had been studying too hard or growing too fast, I cannot say, but while working in the Yard, he fainted. There was nothing organic in the attack and Joe was never again troubled by his heart. The importance of the event lay in the fact that George Grigson happened to be passing at the time. The owner of the yard ordered Joe to be carried into his office and stretched out there upon a bench. In ten minutes Joe had quite recovered. He got up, rather confused under Mr. Grigson's eye, and began to pull on his jacket, which had been bundled to support his head. As he did so, a book fell out of his pocket to the floor, the title plainly visible: *Treatise on the Differential Calculus*. Mr. Grigson's surprised glance traveled from the book to his apprentice. There was a silence. Then Grigson said: "You can knock off now. Come and see me tomorrow at ten o'clock."

Now, George Grigson, a stocky, ruddy-faced man of forty-nine, was, in the local idiom, a "character," known for his heartiness, his quick decisions, his repartees—a strong personality combining the typical Northern attributes of bluntness and shrewdness with a somewhat eccentric vanity. He lived in "bang-up" style in a grandiose villa on the outskirts of the city, dressed in the finest broadcloth, drove every day to the Yard in a brassy De Dion coupé, and at the same time slapped his workers on the back, cursed and conversed with them hail-fellow-well-met, in broad Tyneside.

Such a man was flattered that one of *his* apprentices should be "a dab at mathematics," secretly working for the B.Sc. degree. It added to his own lustre and to that of his Yard (of which he was inordinately proud), and besides, it made a fine after-dinner story. Immediately he had verified Joe's talents—he was not the man to take them on trust—he responded by the appropriate gesture. He promoted Joe from the dungaree squad to a junior position in the drawing office.

With a wage of nearly three pounds a week, Joe took his first decisive step—he left Shalehaven and rented an attic room at Floyd's, a highly respectable boarding-house in River Street. It was a great relief to escape from the drabness of Aunt Sarah's household, nor could he reproach himself for this act of emancipation. Surely he could not be expected to shoulder his aunt's worries all his life. There was no justification for the words of vexation and reproach which she cast at him as, bag in hand, he walked out of the house for good.

At Floyd's, which was well run by Mrs. Floyd, a widow, and her daughter Jenny, Joe had as fellow boarders several of the Grigson draughtsmen and also a number of medical students attending the Armstrong College. Indeed, I was lodging there myself, and I saw a good deal of Joe at this time. He lived very quietly, geared to a painstaking schedule, rising early to shine his shoes and put on his neat blue suit, attending the drawing office with the utmost regularity, retiring to his room every night after our "high tea," which took the place of supper, to study for his degree.

It was difficult to get him to join the rest of us in an evening's entertainment at the Palace Music Hall or the Tyneside Roller Rink. We put him down as being shy, for he scarcely uttered a word at the long table where we all took our meals. In spite of this, Joe was quite a favourite. He had developed into a nice-looking young fellow, with a warm, though slightly worried, smile, and his personality was as modest and engaging as his appearance. Nobody laughed when Sorensen, our big, larky South African student, let out that Joe washed his shirts in his room. We rather esteemed him for this youthful economy—so different from our own careless habits—and when Joe solemnly confided in me that he had started a savings account into which he regularly paid one pound every week, I experienced a spendthrift's throb of envy. Nevertheless, it came as a surprise, one might almost say a shock, when I noticed that Jenny Floyd was beginning to get sweet on Joe.

Jenny, who helped her mother with the housekeeping, was nineteen, an unusually pretty girl—slight and vivacious, with gay brown eyes and curly hair. She was accomplished, too—sang and played the piano nicely, danced and roller-skated, and, in her spare time, had taken the St. John's nursing certificate. Naturally she was the pet of the boarding-house; all we fellows were in love with her. But Jenny was adept at laughing off our attentions, and her buxom, highly respected mother, Ma Floyd, had a hard eye for anyone remotely resembling a masher. I could scarcely believe it when Jenny started blushing as Joe unobtrusively entered the dining-room, and when Ma remarked to me, with her gaze reflectively upon my friend: "He's the steadiest young man I've ever had in my house."

SIGNS OF the favour of the two women gradually surrounded Joe. When he had been twelve months at Floyd's, Ma was taking care of his laundry and his socks. Often, after those Sundays when Jenny had been visiting her cousins in the country, he would find in his room a little vase of sweetbriar or mignonette.

"Joe," I said to him one day. "You're a lucky chap."

He looked up from his book. "What do you mean?"

"Dash it all, man, you must know that Jenny's in love with you. We're all green with envy. You ought to show a little more enthusiasm, unless you don't care a hang for the girl."

"You're quite wrong." His expression became uncomfortable, almost nervous. "I'm very fond of Jenny. Only—"

"Only what?"

"Well, only that I can't do anything about it. You can't propose to a girl on three quid a week."

"It's been done on less."

"Not by me." Joe's face wore the familiar look of strain, of alarmed intensity. "I've got my way to make first. I've seen enough pinching and scraping to last me a lifetime." He returned his eyes resolutely to his book. . . .

At the shipyard, George Grigson was pleased with

the progress of his protégé. True, Joe had done nothing spectacular, but he was quick, obliging, always "on the job" with a silent, earnest desire to succeed, which won the "old man." In the early part of 1912 he transferred Joe to the experimental tank where, by means of wax models and elaborate recording gear, the speeds, strains and stresses of the vessels proposed for construction were tested. At the tank, Joe saw a deal more of his patron, under circumstances of greater intimacy—both, for instance, would be down on their knees together, on the edge of the tank, watching the behaviour of a model under test, sharing the exhilaration of success or the dejection, spiced with companionable profanity from the boss, of failure.

MORE AND more Grigson came to utilize Joe, shouting for him the length of the office, often sending him in the car to his residence for something he had forgotten, or to convey some message to his wife. In this fashion Joe came to meet Mrs. Grigson, a stout, overdressed, stupid, but immensely good-natured woman who usually received him in lacy mob caps and feathery morning gowns, who scarcely knew whether to tip Joe or offer him a drink, and who compromised by pressing on him chocolates from the box which always stood open by the sofa in her drawing-room.

It flattered Grigson that "the missus" should like his young man. He raised Joe's salary to four pounds ten a week. Finally, on the day Joe took his B.Sc. at the Armstrong College, Grigson, greatly pleased, signalized the occasion by inviting him to dinner. As though regretting this lapse of dignity, he added gruffly: "There'll be only the missus and me."

It was a distinct step forward for Joe to be invited socially to his employer's home, and nervously he took pains to make himself as presentable as possible. When he reached the stucco mansion in its pretentious suburban garden, his knees felt weak. Nor was his confusion lessened by the appearance at dinner—quite contrary to Grigson's prediction—of the daughter of the house. This was Ada, who had come home a few days earlier than expected, from her expensive finishing school at Nognor in the South of England, because of an outbreak of chickenpox amongst the younger girls.

At first the atmosphere of the dinner table was stiff—Grigson, who idolized his daughter, plainly chafed at this intrusion of an outsider upon their reunion. But Joe, with his eyes on his plate, was obviously so anxious to please and to avoid obtruding himself, so fearful, too, of using the wrong fork from amongst the array of cutlery before him, that Grigson began to thaw. Always fond of his food, his mood was further softened by the rich succulent dinner, and by the time the dessert was served he had slapped Joe on the back.

"Drink your champagne, man. Our Ada won't bite you!"

FRANKLY, Ada did not quite know what to make of Joe. She was a plump, medium-sized girl with china-blue eyes and fine flaxen hair who would one day precisely resemble her obese mamma. Now, however, although her red lips often took on a petulant fullness, she was youthful and appealing, indulged rather than spoiled, innocent yet amorous. Her first impulse had been to laugh at Joe—he was so awkward, so absurdly worried. But as she studied his pale, regular features, encountered his shy gray eyes and was rewarded finally by his diffident yet warm smile, a queer thrill pervaded her. He was an interesting young man, she decided, and the circumstances surrounding him were romantic. He reminded her of Julien Sorel, the hero of "Le Rouge et le Noir," a forbidden book which she had read avidly in her dormitory cubicle. That night, as she brushed her hair, admiring her pink-and-white complexion in the mirror, she realized that he attracted her.

Joe was genuinely astonished, in the weeks which followed, to find himself the object of Ada's attentions. He had no conceit whatsoever, and it took a series of invitations to convince him that the boss's daughter was smitten with him. In that summer of 1914, before the outbreak of the war, there was, even in a provincial city like Tynecastle, a sense of crisis which expressed itself in a queer kind of hectic gaiety. Ada's circle of young people raced around, and somehow Ada saw to it that Joe came with them.

Every meeting served to increase her feeling for him, and presently she was taking him driving in her runabout in the cool of the evening. Or they would drop into a quiet cinema, just the two of them, and hold hands in the darkness. At the party given to Ada for her eighteenth birthday, she danced every foxtrot with him.

At first Joe felt flattered by this intensity; then he became rather scared. No wonder he took special pains to avoid Jenny's eye in the dining-room at Floyd's. He had never committed himself with Jenny, yet surely, despite his cautious nature, a tacit understanding had existed between them. Jenny had heard about Ada, of course. She almost ignored Joe now, and her little attentions, like the placing of flowers in his room, abruptly ceased.

One night I was on the landing when Jenny passed Joe upon the stairs. Only a faint light was burning, and neither of them observed me as, almost involuntarily, they stopped.

"Well," Joe said, "I haven't seen much of you lately."

"No, Joe." A sudden quiver was evident in Jenny's voice. "I've missed you."

A silence followed. Jenny's face was upturned; one could guess that she was ready to forgive. But Joe didn't kiss her. Some strange inner force held him back. Instead, he mumbled: "I don't like the look of the German situation." Then he went on, clumsily, up the stairs, and into his room.

The following week, war was declared. By a lucky chance I had passed my final examinations, and, with Sorensen and some others in my class, I joined the RAMC. Jenny, who had her first-aid certificate, volunteered for nursing duty. Joe, being at the Yard, was in a deferred occupation.

But events were moving swiftly—not only in the cosmic crisis, but also in Joe's private drama, for suddenly the full story of Ada's infatuation was brought to the notice of her father. Of course, Grigson was furious. He sent for Joe and in a violent scene accused him of everything from rank ingratitude to attempted abduction. Joe took it very well. I think he was glad, in a way, that the situation should come to a head. He went home to his lodgings, wrote an emotional letter to Grigson which contained the memorable phrase "Of course, sir, I could never afford to support Ada in the luxury to which she is accustomed..." then went out and joined the Navy.

Months passed—I was in France, Jenny had been posted to the naval hospital at Malta, Joe was minesweeping on the North Sea. Meanwhile, George Grigson's rage cooled off. Joe's apology had greatly mollified him; he often referred to it as "a damn fine letter." Also, he had before him, day in and day out, a lovesick daughter, refusing to be comforted, abetted by a mother whose every glance accused him of sending a hero to his doom.

Grigson was a hard man, but this petticoat influence gradually wore him down. When the war ended and Joe returned, very smart in his uniform, he was taken back, with acclamation, to the Grigson Yard. After that, the matter was never in doubt. Grigson, as I have said, was fond of Joe, his ideas were essentially democratic, and when he saw finally that Ada's mind was made up, he summoned Joe to his office, offered to make him a junior partner in two years' time, then concluded in his broad Tyneside: "I'm a damn fool, Joe, to let ye in on this. But our Ada wants ye, and there's an end on't."

JOE WALKED out, dazzled by his prospects. With a surge of gratitude, his tenderness toward Ada increased. He quickly fell in with the arrangements for the elaborate wedding which Ada and her mother were planning for the coming June. He smiled complacently at all the fittings and fussings which went with the preparation of Ada's elaborate trousseau, and obediently removed himself from the drawing-room, which now looked like a millinery salon, when, with a fond and meaning glance, Ada prepared for a new "try-on." His elation might have remained undimmed if, about a week before the wedding, Jenny had not arrived home, gay and pretty as ever, but with a new charm which made her more attractive than before.

Joe was a good fellow, conscientiously in love with Ada; nevertheless, he could not quite get Jenny out of his mind. One evening, on his way back from work, about a fortnight before the date of the wedding, he encountered her in Tynecastle High Street. He stopped, then, on an impulse and asked her to have tea with him in the Castle Café, "for old times' sake." With an odd smile, she accepted. During tea they talked of ordinary things, of her experiences in Malta and later in Italy and France. Suddenly, looking him full in the face, that same half smile on her lips, she said: "Travel's a wonderful thing, Joe. Don't you ever want to get on a liner and set out for a new country—America, maybe? It might be fun if you had someone with you who didn't bore you."

Joe went white. It was impossible to mistake her meaning, or the challenge in her eyes. For a moment a wild desire swept over him. Why not? He had five hundred pounds in the bank—he had always adored Jenny—why deny it?—she had always been the one he wanted. What did it matter if they were hard up? He reached out toward her ungloved hand, near him. Then, all at once, he remembered Ada, the Yard, and most of all the partnership in two years' time. A constriction narrowed his throat, a cold fear that seemed to come from far back in his life, from his ragged childhood in Shalehaven. He was still, at heart, a poor boy; he could not afford to throw away his prospects, his safe and settled future. His eyes fell, and after a moment he mumbled an excuse.

"It's getting late, Jenny. Time we were going."

EVERYONE AGREED it was a nice wedding; Joe looked so purposeful, Ada so young and blooming. After the honeymoon, which was spent in the

Lake District, the young couple settled down in a bijou residence in Laurel Avenue, only half a mile from the Grigson estate. Do not imagine that Joe suffered disillusionment in his marriage. On the contrary, he was well content. Ada's youthful love stirred and gratified him; he had a pleasant home and unexampled prospects; often he asked himself what better fortune a man could desire. True, he sometimes found the social excitement which Ada loved something of a penance; it was tiresome to have people to the house, or to go out on a chilly night, when he would have preferred his cozy fireside and a book. Then Mrs. Grigson, in her maternal devotion, was a nuisance. But his greatest trouble centered in Ada's extravagance.

Joe now had a salary of seven hundred a year, Ada had pin-money of her own, and of course there was always the comfortable feeling that her father stood behind her. Nevertheless, Ada had been extravagantly brought up; she loved pretty things, especially clothes, and could deny herself nothing. Moreover, she was not a good housekeeper; her servants, and the tradesmen with whom she dealt, imposed upon her. When the bills came in, Joe turned pale, and taking Ada aside, he gave her many pained, though loving, lectures on the principles of economy. He explained that he was a simple man, with very simple tastes. Starting out on life, as they were, the important thing—here Joe's voice took on an impassioned seriousness—was to save money, to build up for the future.

It was difficult to reason with a playful wife who insisted upon sitting upon his knee, and who terminated his arguments by putting her soft arms round his neck. She had not been listening, anyway. Nevertheless, she did try, in her own way. It did no good at all, and when she became embarrassed, rather than annoy Joe, she went to her father, who could deny her nothing but who, for once, smiled rather grimly as he handed her the cheque. Joe, in the meantime, assiduously practiced what he preached. He always saved money out of the allowance set aside for his personal needs, and he found it a real pleasure to shut himself in his study every Sunday afternoon to balance the figures in his little black book. It gave him a thrill when his savings reached the thousand-pound mark. His only embarrassments were the presents which Ada periodically gave him—articles like silk dressing-gowns and elaborate smoking-cabinets, which he did not really want and which cost a lot of money.

At the Yard, Joe's relations with his father-in-law continued satisfactorily. Perhaps Grigson was less jovial, less communicative than before—Joe often noticed a harassed contraction of the lines around his eyes. But then, he was growing older, and certainly business was less good than it had been during the war. Long lines of vessels were laid up in the Tyne, their hulls slowly rusting, for lack of trade. A fortunate contract for two South American boats kept

Grigson's going, but the other yards were feeling the pinch.

Then, in the third year of her marriage, Ada became pregnant, and everyone, especially old Grigson, who had set his heart on a grandson, was delighted. I must not dwell upon the pleased anticipation of the family, on Joe's solicitude, on all the preparations which were made for the event.

However, through one of those tragic chances which occur, in spite of every care, something went wrong with Ada's confinement. The child was stillborn, and, two days later, Ada died.

Joe was stunned, completely unmanned; for weeks he existed in a state of stupefied misery. He was staying, for the time being, with the Grigsons, and more than once he laid his head on his mother-in-law's tremendous bosom and wept. For weeks after the funeral, his sentimental grief drew him to the cemetery, where, in the evenings, he would linger at Ada's grave. Gradually, however, he pulled himself together—there were many things that were demanding his attention.

FIRST, HE sold the house in Laurel Avenue—he could not bear to live in it; besides, a widower had no need of such an establishment. Then, for similar reasons, he disposed of the furniture, fittings and carpets, also the garden implements. Prices were high at that period, and the sum realized was considerable—the big double bed alone brought full seventy pounds, which was five pounds more than Ada had paid for it. When the fuss of the auctions was over, Joe took a room at the Tyneside Union Club and threw himself into his work at the Yard in an effort to forget.

He was beginning to be afraid that he might not get his partnership. After all, there was no obligation upon Mr. Grigson to fulfill his promise, since the foundation upon which it was based, his being married to Ada, no longer existed. He redoubled his attentions to Mr. Grigson, went to revival meetings with his mother-in-law, who in her sorrow had found religion; he grew very close to them indeed. Covertly studying the old man's face of an evening, across the chequer board, he would try to discover how he stood with him. Grigson had changed considerably; he had become moody, intolerant, careless of his appearance, and often he was alarmingly rude to Joe.

A year passed in this fashion, and Joe's anxiety became acute—he was still merely the manager of the drawing office and quite outside the real affairs of the firm. More than once it was on the tip of his tongue to ask the question which meant so much to him, but always his natural prudence and the fear of a calamitous rebuff deterred him.

Then, one Sunday afternoon, about eighteen months after Ada's death, Grigson took Joe into his library and himself broached the subject. It was a hot summer afternoon; the mutton at midday dinner had been greasy and indigestible; the sun streaming through the window, where a fly was buzzing, revealed little patches of dust on the upper edges of leather-bound volumes which were never opened. From an adjoining room came the thin, melancholy notes of a hymn picked out by Mrs. Grigson on the harmonium. Sunk in his leather armchair, the old man clasped his hands upon his stomach and fixed his eye on Joe. His tone was affectionate, even gentle.

"You've been worrying a lot lately about that deed of partnership, Joe?"

Joe reddened and stammered a reply.

"Well, I wouldn't if I were you. You could have it tomorrow if you wished. But it wouldn't be worth the paper it was written on."

He began, methodically, to outline the circumstances of his failure. Always uncommunicative, he now spared no detail of the catastrophe, while Joe stared, aghast, scarcely believing what he heard. The slump in shipping had been bad enough, yet they might have weathered it, had they not committed themselves to these South American boats. To get this order, while the other shipyards stood idle, Grigson had borrowed heavily, mortgaged every nut, bolt and rivet in the yard. And now the company in South America was in liquidation.

JOE STILL could not assimilate it—this assertive man, who had held his head so high, and taken such pride in the prestige of his yard, could not possibly be reduced to nothing. Indeed, it struck him that his father-in-law might well be pulling the wool over his ears from motives of personal expediency. He left the house in a dither of uncertainty.

Next day, his doubts were set aside. While inspecting the top derrick of the empty drydock, George Grigson missed his footing and fell ninety feet to the concrete pier beneath. He was killed instantly—a tragic slip. But Joe believed that it was no accident. Old George had preferred not to witness his own ruin.

This event affected Joe almost as deeply as the death of Ada. The whole perspective of his life was shattered. He felt that nowhere could security be found. His fear of destitution, which for many years had only troubled him subconsciously, now became an open dread. He could not bear to remain at the Yard. Even before the official receiver took over and sealed the big gates, Joe had packed up and departed. The same impulse of flight caused him to give up his comfortable quarters at the Union Club. In his extremity he gravitated, curiously enough, to his old room at Floyd's. Here, like a badger gone to earth, he was able to examine his situation.

This stock-taking showed some things which were good and others that were bad. His capital was not far short of four thousand pounds; he had the B.Sc. degree, plus a thorough knowledge of draughtsmanship, and, although shaken, sound bodily health. Against this, he saw little prospect for himself as a marine architect, nor was it likely that he would again find a patron prepared to expedite his advancement. In any case, he recoiled from the mere idea of building ships. At the same time, he did not wish to enter a blind alley by accepting a mediocre salaried post.

In this dilemma, he met in with Sam Netley, a Shalehaven man who was now a master mason in Tynecastle. Netley was more than ten years older than Joe, a slow but reliable character, who did odd-jobbing work and conducted a small business in granite monuments, chiefly tombstones. He lived obscurely with his aged mother and sister in a little stone house adjoining his corrugated-iron builder's sheds, seemingly well content to plod along on his earnings of five pounds a week and to raise prize bantams as a hobby.

But Joe had other ideas. He knew that although ships might be at a discount, houses were in high demand; in fact, an acute housing shortage existed all over Tyneside. It was a dreadful ordeal for Joe to risk his capital, but he had weighed the chances, and it was now or never. In partnership with Netley, he drew up plans, bought three acres of land, and proceeded to erect three houses on a new arterial road. Joe had scant knowledge of building, but such was his anxiety, he took off his coat and worked with Netley and his men, mixing mortar, trucking bricks, even carrying a hod like a common labourer.

Within nine months the houses were finished, within nine days they were sold, and Joe and Netley had cleared a profit of over three thousand pounds. Of this sum Joe, who had put up the capital, took two thousand, while Netley, who had merely supplied the experience, received one. Even so, Sam Netley was delighted, full of admiration for Joe's enterprise, and eager to repeat the experience. They bought another strip of frontage on the same road and started work on another three dwellings.

Meantime, Joe continued living at Floyd's—he explained that he found it cheap and convenient. Yet perhaps he had another reason. For the past three years, Jenny Floyd had been nursing in London; she was now a staff sister in St. Thomas' Hospital; and when, in the summer of 1924, she came home on leave, Joe looked like a man whose patience had at last been rewarded. He blossomed out, bought himself a new suit, and actually was seen smoking a cigar. For a few days he was discreetly friendly, but on Saturday afternoon he asked her to accompany him for a stroll, and, as they passed the Castle Café, he suggested with a rather sheepish air that they drop in for tea.

This was an important moment for Joe, a unique moment which should he noted in his history—he was actually doing something which he wished to do, something not dictated by prudence or policy or the subconscious phobias of his youth. In the tearoom, he asked Jenny to marry him.

Jenny lowered her gaze, then raised it again toward Joe. He was just thirty and looked younger; not handsome, of course, but, in the Tyneside idiom, "a well-favoured chap," with a clear fair skin and nice chestnut hair. Since he never ate much, his figure was still spare and boyish. His eyes, with their diffident, troubled expression, were particularly appealing.

There was a pause; then she shook her head slowly.

"I'm sorry, Joe. You're a bit late."

She had once been in love with Joe, but now there remained only a faint fondness, inexplicably mixed with pity. Quietly she told him that she was marrying a doctor with whom she had been working at St. Thomas'. They were leaving for Cape Town, where his father had bought him a practice. She could not forbear concluding, with a queer smile:

"It's fun to travel, when you're with someone you like."

AFTER THIS, Joe did not stay long at Floyd's—it was less convenient than he had believed. However, he did not return to the Union Club, but went to live with his partner, Sam Netley, who for weeks had pressed Joe to make use of the spare bedroom, with the parlor, which was never used, as his sitting-room. This was a step down from Laurel Avenue—the parlor had red plush furniture, wax flowers on the mantelpiece and an aspidistra in the window—but it was quite congenial to Joe; he felt comfortable and at home there.

Joe, in fact, was much impressed by the efficiency with which Belle Netley, Sam's sister, managed the household, single-handed. Belle was a short, plain, taciturn, sternly energetic person of twenty-four. She looked exactly what she was—a working girl—and she spent most of her day in a blue print wrapper, her hair tied in an old red handkerchief, cooking, washing, scrubbing, attending to her bedridden mother, keeping the house as clean and shining as a new pin.

Sam, to do him justice, often pleaded with her to have "help," but Belle, with her level, unsmiling regard, always contemptuously shook her head. She was strong, splendidly healthy, and so far as could be judged, took a proud satisfaction in her domestic prowess. Her cooking was far and away the best Joe had ever tasted—not fancy, mind you—but plain working-class dishes, like steak and kidney pie or jellied eels or silverside and dumplings, creations from which the mere aroma made Joe and Sam exchange a smile and smack their lips as they sat down together at table in their shirt-sleeves, while Belle stood waiting to serve them, watching for, yet calmly confident of, their approval. When Joe, sitting back, would exclaim: "By gum, Belle, that was a champion stew," a calm suspicion of a smile might suffuse her homely face, completely innocent of make-up, the cheekbones reddened, the lips chapped; then, with a matter-of-fact nod, she would step into the scullery to fetch him his dessert.

What made her housekeeping the more remarkable was the absolute economy with which she achieved it. Not only did she get the best value in the local stores—no tradesman ever took advantage of her—

but with a two-penny nap bone and a handful of mixed vegetables she could produce a soup not to be equaled at the Ritz.

Although Joe's eye strayed occasionally in an absent, masculine fashion over Belle's strong haunches and firm ankles, it must be admitted that he never really thought of her as a woman. She was too plain, too completely devoid of coquetry. But when, eight months later, old Mrs. Netley passed away peacefully upstairs, a curious reaction occurred in Joe. Perhaps he was sorry for Belle—although there was no great occasion for compassion, since the consensus of local opinion rated the event as "a happy release"—perhaps her new black dress, tight round the bust, showing her fine contours, gave her suddenly an unfamiliar aspect, not unattractive, in his eyes.

At any rate, one evening, about ten days after the funeral, while Sam was out attending an Odd Fellows' meeting, Joe stood at the back porch enjoying the warm spring twilight. Across the back yard, in the shed, Belle was busy with a bale of hay which had been delivered that afternoon for Sam's famous bantams. On an impulse, Joe strolled over to help her. How it happened he never knew, but the next minute he had her in his arms.

When he came to himself, Joe's confusion and consternation were extreme—he scarcely dared move or speak. Then, in the darkness, he heard Belle's calm and practical voice: "I better go in now, or the broth on the stove will singe." Joe hung about the back yard for a long time; then, gazing up at the stars, he slapped his thigh and muttered between relief and admiration: "What a woman!"

Any lingering fears that he had ruined his comfortable way of life were soon dispelled. Belle's attitude remained stoically unchanged. Sam, of course, suspected nothing. Occasionally Joe gave Belle little presents—a silk scarf, a leather handbag, a wicker-fitted work basket—but while she thanked him, she never seemed to want them.

THE PARTNERSHIP between Joe and Netley continued profitable for the next two years. Then, one day, as they sat down at the parlor table to consider a new tract that seemed ripe for development, Sam suddenly said: "No."

He puffed at his pipe and went on: "The boom's over, Joe. There's houses and to spare. Them that goes on speculating will burn their fingers."

Joe was silent; then he nodded reflectively.

"I believe you're right, Sam. We'll get out of housing and into general construction. The Empire Theaters are going to put up a new music hall on Tyne Street. Tenders invited by the end of next month. We could put in for that, Sam."

Sam shook his head. "You go ahead if you like, Joe. But I'm out. I've made eight thousand quid, and that's enough. If I had more, I'd not know what to do wi't. I've bought a poultry farm back on Alnwick Moor. I'm going up there to have some fun before I die."

Joe stared at Netley, nonplused. He simply could not understand why a man not yet fifty, hale and hearty, should wish to retire to a farm, when he was making money hand over fist. Eight thousand pounds was little enough. Why, he himself was worth thirty thousand and that was only the beginning. Ht gave his partner a last chance. "I wish you'd change your mind. Sam."

"No, Joe. Everything's fixed. You tender for the new Empire on your own. And good luck to you, lad."

The next few weeks were filled with Sam's preparations for departure. Joe took over the sheds and scaffolding, and all the stores and equipment, at a fair valuation. The house was to be let at the end of the quarter, for, of course, Belle was accompanying her brother to the farm.

In a way Joe was glad to be escaping so easily. He had submitted an estimate for the proposed new music hall, but the result would not be known for another month. He felt free, but restless and at a loose end.

It was Belle who suggested, calmly, that he should take a holiday—a cruise to the Mediterranean would do him good. In his present mood, Joe was ready to agree. Why not? He had earned the right to a little relaxation. The sailing lists showed that a boat was leaving the following week—not one of the best ships of its line; one of the smaller and less commodious vessels, but that meant the fare was correspondingly reduced. Thirty pounds return to the island he had selected—a saving of nearly ten pounds! Joe paid for his ticket, and on the day that Sam and Belle left for the farm, he took the train to Liverpool and went on board. During the railway journey he felt slightly aggrieved that Belle had not shown some emotion when she said good-by.

The cruise failed to fulfill his expectations. The passengers were mainly uninteresting tourists who engaged in rowdy deck games, and Joe, disillusioned, kept much to himself. In this reserve his example was followed by a lady, traveling alone with her maid. Her name did not appear on the passenger list, and wrapped in a gray rug, she reclined in a deck chair in a nook by the ventilators, her gaze sometimes lighting upon him, over the edge of her novel, with, he sensed, a half-humorous sympathy. She was slightly over thirty, tall and slender, with fine wrists and hands, rather pale, which perhaps accounted for the sadness of her expression in repose, with beautiful, ironic yet animated, eyes.

Driven by his loneliness, Joe raised his cap and spoke to her. She smiled, in unaffected friendliness.

"We seem to be the two pariahs of this ship. Won't you join me?"

The deck steward brought another chair. Later that day, Joe was startled to learn from the purser that she was Lady Irene Mostray, widow of Captain Hugo Mostray of the Grenadier Guards, and the third daughter of the Earl of Brantham.

IN SPITE of the instinctive awe aroused in Joe by this information, their friendship progressed. Everything about her impressed and fascinated him. Her charm, culture and, above all, her breeding, which shone through every gesture, every word, every inflection of her voice, were a revelation to him. Her witty comments upon the prevailing gambols, uttered with complete repose but with a satiric sparkle in her eye, made him laugh.

Then she laughed, too, for in the enforced tedium of this voyage, he amused and interested her. His naturally attractive personality had never shown to better advantage than when he told her, simply and with that touch of sentiment which he always displayed toward his boyhood, of his humble origin and early struggles, of his rise to success. There was a longish silence when he concluded, filled by the sounding of the blue water against the bows. "Here," she reflected, "is a real man."

Her married life had not been happy. Her husband, remnant of a long and washed-out line, had been a waster, who had run through his property and her own. Annoyed with herself, she shook away an absurd fancy. Yet on the evening of the fifth day, as a faint landfall crept up on the luminous sea, she turned to Joe with real regret.

"I've enjoyed meeting you so much. I'm sorry we shall say good-by tomorrow."

"But we have the voyage home."

She smiled and shook her head, gathering up her rug. "I couldn't bear it on this ship. Marie and I shall stop ashore for a week and take the next homeward P. and O." She named the hotel where she would stop.

"But," Joe protested, "you'll lose your return fare."

Rising, she still smiled, yet her eyebrows lifted slightly, and at that silent, imperceptible rebuke Joe blushed violently, painfully—he scarcely knew why. He paced the deck late that night, and, aggravated and disturbed, reached a decision which remained unshaken even when a protracted interview with the purser on the subject of a refund of passage-money proved unsuccessful. The following morning, when they dropped anchor, he went ashore, looking supremely casual, in the second launch, and ordered his baggage to be sent to the hotel Lady Irene had named.

Lady Irene made no comment upon his appearance; she seemed genuinely pleased to see him. And during the next three days they spent much time together, exploring the quaint side streets of the town, viewing the native lace-makers at work in doorways festooned with purple bougainvillaea, taking their meals alfresco in odd little open-air cafés near the fountain playing in the cool square. As they strolled back to the hotel in the flower-scented dusk, jeweled by flitting fireflies, lightly, she took his arm.

On the fourth day a P. and O. liner came into the

bay, and as inquiry revealed that the next available boat would not arrive until three weeks later. Lady Irene decided she must return. So, indeed, did Joe. As he stood on the veranda with her, while Marie packed her valises, he experienced a peculiar exhilaration—a mood foreign to him, and almost unreal. At that moment, however, when he might have spoken, the manager appeared to present her bill and to declare that since Lady Irene had affirmed her intention of staying a week, she must pay for that full period.

JOE took the bill and examined it. He saw, with indignation, that it was preposterous: four days extra, not only for the suite, but for meals and table wine, as well.

"It's ridiculous." He said to Irene: "I'll not let you pay it."

"You will pay," the manager interposed offensively. "Or I shall call the police."

Joe turned upon the short, olive-skinned manager. He knew a "try-on" when he saw one, and he had the measure of his man. In broad Tyneside, he swore that he would have the hotel blacklisted with every British travel agency. He used the words "fraud" and "extortion." The manager wilted; his gestures grew more profuse. He was cringing, on the verge of an apology, when suddenly, with a gesture of disgust, Lady Irene opened her bag and threw some notes upon the table.

"Take it," she said curtly. "And go."

Dead silence, while the manager backed and

bowed himself out. Joe bit his lip, staring at the floor.

"Oh, well," he shrugged at last. "I suppose it's all right if you can afford it."

She smiled faintly, and touching his arm to show she was not ungrateful, she replied:

"My dear friend, if you must know, I am rather badly off. But I have found that the only possible attitude toward money is to treat it with contempt."

He had nothing to say. Nor, during the trip home, did he once mention the subject. But he thought of it frequently with baffled, knitted brows.

WHEN JOE got back to Tynecastle, he found on his desk the rejected tender for the Empire contract. Undeterred, he immediately submitted an estimate for the new head offices of a large company. Here, perhaps because the project was less ambitious and more suited to his resources, he was successful. He mustered his men and, with the energy of one who feels he has lately been wasting his time, set to work.

Yet while he worked, his thoughts kept flying back provokingly to his elegant and aristocratic traveling companion. Confound it, was he in love with her? Not since he had known Jenny had he experienced such an upsetting emotion. And this was more intense, more complex, combining longing, admiration, respect, with a maddening admixture of timidity. What aggravated the disturbance was the impression, conveyed through her faintly ironic, well-bred reserve, that she cared for him. Before they parted she had asked him to visit her at Wooton Downs, her "little country place" in Sussex. He stood off the impulse as long as he could, but once the back of the new construction work was broken, he suddenly yielded, booked a seat on the Southern express, and wired her to expect him for the weekend.

Irene met him at the station, bareheaded and in tweeds, and drove him in a neat pony carriage. An early summer had caused the sweet countryside to burgeon. As they came up the long avenue, an evening mist was gathering about the tall elms where rooks circled and cawed, lending greater mystery to the aged place, giving to the low, red-tiled house added dignity and beauty. Though Joe was not schooled in such matters, he judged this to be a rare and lovely specimen of Tudor architecture. It was very run-down, of course—even in the fading light he could discern a weather vane blown off, a drooping coping, a lack of paint on the stable doors, an air of raggedness about the old yew hedges. But it was charming and distinguished—yes, distinguished as the woman at his side.

They dined by candlelight. Irene's youngest sister was staying in the house, and an old manservant, rather doddery, but with a perfect demeanour, served a simple dinner to the three of them. Joe slept well in a paneled room, and next morning, which was warm and sunny, Irene took him walking round the place.

It exhilarated him to be with her again, and she, looking younger than before, seemed equally glad to see him. As they swung along side by side, the nearness of her slender limbs gave him a swift, darkly warm appreciation of the delight that intimacy with so fastidious a woman would bring to any man.

Yet as the day wore on, he was conscious of a growing anxiety, amounting almost to an apprehension. This alarm arose from nothing that she said, for her speech, as always, was quietly restrained, but rather from an invitation, a message, only half hidden, in her comradely glances. It was, in fact, an offering of herself to him, together with this lovely but half-ruined estate, which, using his enterprise and means, they would restore together. Her frank affection made no secret of how they might materially help each other. In return for his generosity she could offer him social position, introduce him to a society he could not otherwise have known, use her influence to further his ambitions. Here they might entertain, fittingly, the best in the land. There was no limit to what they might attain.

Late in the afternoon, as they returned, coming through the Italian water garden, overgrown with lilies, and across the paddocks, so that she might give a carrot to the pony, she flashed him a shy and, for once, quite tremulous smile.

"It would be fun to have hunters here again. I love to ride, and I'm sure you would, too." She paused, striving unsuccessfully for her ironic note. "It's one of the things one gives up, dear friend, when one has scarcely got a bean."

Fun? Yes, indeed, it might be the greatest fun. In spite of his fear, Joe was terribly tempted.

That night he tossed restlessly in his paneled room. Irene was a beautiful, desirable woman—a lady, by gum—and she loved him. He saw himself her husband, master of this place, hobnobbing with her father, the Earl, and riding to hounds in a red tailcoat. Then he groaned out loud: "No, no—a thousand times no." He couldn't do it—it would take five thousand a year to run this place, and a cool ten thousand to put it on its feet. Then look at the servants they'd need, the gardeners, the keeper, the bailiff for the home farm. Probably Irene's relations would sponge on him eternally. . . . No, that wasn't true; Irene was a thoroughbred, would never stand for such a thing. . . . Yet hadn't she hinted that her young sister might go to a Swiss boarding-school?"

Joe groaned again. It wasn't that he doubted his ability to make enough money. He knew that he could, but he could not bring himself to squander it in so prodigal a fashion. It wasn't his style; he was just a working lad, a poor boy who had worn bursted boots and known the pinch of hunger. Mind you, if this had happened to him in another ten years, when he had really consolidated his finances, amassed an unassailable fortune, he would have jumped, simply jumped at it. But not now. . . . Oh, no, for pity's sake, not now.

At first signs of dawn, Joe rose and packed his bag, hurriedly scrawled a note saying that he was required urgently at his office, then tiptoed out of the house. All the way to the station that last half-tremulous smile of Irene's tormented him, but once he was in the train he gave a gasp of relief. He reached Tynecastle at four in the afternoon, and, telephoning for his car, he drove straight out to Sam Netley's farm. Belle was in the spotless kitchen, in her wrapper, preparing the high tea. Joe's nostrils expanded to the rich odour of black puddings. He strode over to Belle and put his arms roughly round her.

"Eh, lass," he said. "You and me'll wed."

THEY WERE married the week after the completion of the new offices, an enterprise which netted Joe 3,750 pounds—somewhat less than he had calculated, for he had been obliged to buy his bricks on a rising market, but still, a tidy sum. They spent a honeymoon week at an old family hotel in Blackpool, and although Joe had been a little nervous as to how Belle might conduct herself, he soon was reassured. Quiet in her dress, adaptable in her deportment, Belle also knew when to keep her mouth shut. She had no frills about her, yet she knew "what was what," and occasionally made Joe chuckle in their room at night with an impassive remark bearing on some fussy or pretentious fellow guest.

It was Belle's sound common sense which dissuaded Joe from his intention to set up in Sam's old house by the building yard. She protested that it was not "up to" his new position in business; besides, she wanted better plumbing and a modern kitchen. So they took over one of the eight-roomed villas which Joe had built himself, and, with all the confidence of a man aware that he has a dependable and economical partner at home, Joe flung himself even more zestfully into business.

He was now accepted as a prominent builder and contractor in the district. He had no artistic satisfaction in the work; it was a "practical proposition," simply a means to an end. . . .

In the next few years he did well. He was, as I have said, a most likeable fellow, who made friends easily. Unlike poor George Grigson, whose assertiveness had instinctively aroused opposition, Joe, with his quiet amiability, had few enemies. He soon was awarded new contracts. More and more he went into "steel."

Yet, while his business expanded into large undertakings, nothing was too small for Joe to handle. He kept a couple of young architects busy on his minor constructions. And if one of his less well-off neighbors came along and asked him, rather hesitantly, to "run up" a fifty-pound garage in his back yard, Joe clapped him on the shoulder and did a good job. A profit, even if it was only five pounds, was always a profit.

Joe was so busy that, except perhaps for an odd day off, he had no time to take a holiday. During this period, to his great joy, two sons were born to him, and although as the summers came round he sent them off with Belle to the seaside, or more often to Sam's farm on the Alnwick Moor, he rarely had leisure to accompany them. "Next year," he would say, with his harassed smile, when they begged him to come. But when next year arrived, more often than not he had another business preoccupation upon his mind.

Really, it was a pity, for Joe now had few distractions. He ate very moderately, seldom drank or smoked, rarely visited the Club. He neither fished nor, unlike Sam, who had become a crack rabbit hunter, went out with the gun. It became quite a business to get him to his tailor. He would answer Belle quizzically: "A man like me can afford to wear old clothes." And he would add, passing his arm round her waist: "I like them as well as I do my old dutch."

Yes, time and again, he recognized with satisfaction that he had made no mistake in marrying Belle—she might not be exciting, yet she was thrifty, undemanding, sensible. Of course she did not, like a fool, maintain her early level of frugality. She now had a maid in the house, and a weekly woman for the laundry. She dressed the children warmly and well. Her own wardrobe contained a nice dark dress for the dinners and official functions to which Joe and she were occasionally invited. But she still knitted socks for Joe and her boys, cooked them tasty dishes, dosed them when they were sick, poulticed away their chills. Beyond a new electric iron or a modern washing-machine, she had never asked Joe for anything in her life. He often calculated, in his study, that she ran his household, and ran it well, on less than five hundred pounds a year. And he was making, on an average, fifteen thousand per annum.

ON HER thirty-fifth birthday, carried away by an access of sentiment, he approached her as she sat knitting, and dropped a crisp paper dramatically in her lap. It was a Tynecastle city bond for one thousand pounds.

"It's for you, lass," he said emotionally. "You're worth it a hundred times over."

She gazed at it calmly, then handed it back to him. "What would I do with that? Put it back in your box, my man, with all the others."

He stood, petrified, unable to believe his ears. Then he embraced her more feelingly than ever before. What a woman! To ease his conscience for accepting back the bond, he opened a savings account for each of his boys. Now that they were growing up, six and eight years old, respectively, it was time for them to learn the value of money.

Joe's success continued—everything he touched seemed to prosper. When he was a little ragged boy, he had dreamed of the days when he might have five hundred pounds. As a young man, he had adjusted the figure to five thousand. Ten years later, he had told himself that fifty thousand would make him independent, secure for life. Yet now that he had far surpassed that sum, he still was not satisfied or at peace. Figuring in his little black book, behind the locked door of his office, he worried about the danger of inflation. The price of everything was going up. Tea, sugar and butter had all risen in price. Even the daily paper now cost double. As for taxes—these were Joe's especial nightmare; the amounts he had to pay nearly broke his heart.

One day, after signing an especially large check, he took his troubles to his old friend Sam, who, in his shirt-sleeves, was grooming a bantam for the poultry show.

"These swine, Sam," he groaned, following a long diatribe against the Revenue Commissioners. "They've stripped me clean."

Sam went on brushing, chirping to the bird. "Ah, lad," he said, carelessly. "You still have summat in your sock."

Joe reddened violently, and, although not given to oaths, he swore indignantly at Sam. "Damn it, man. Don't talk like a fool!"

He went home, sorely vexed, burning with a sense of outrage. As he came up the drive of his villa, he noticed that the electric light had been left on in the tool-shed, which his sons now used as a workroom. The blood rushed to Joe's head. Almost certainly the light had been burning all day long.

When the boys returned from school, he was waiting for them at the gate. "Which of you two left the light on in the tool-shed?"

They glanced at each other uncertainly; then the

elder answered.

"Probably it was me, Father. I was in there doing my fretwork last night."

"Last night!" Joe exclaimed angrily. "Nearly eighteen hours! That means you've wasted a whole unit of electricity."

"I'm sorry."

Then the smaller boy chipped in: "A unit only costs sixpence, Father."

"*Only* sixpence!" Joe struggled with his emotion. "Why, when I was a youngster sixpence was a fortune. I never had one penny, let alone six, to throw away."

He broke off then; even as he glared at them, he melted. They were fine boys, the older boy nearly fourteen—fine, clever, upstanding lads, attending the best school in town, certain to do him credit. He put an arm round each of them and walked with them up to the house.

"You see, boys," he began, in a tender, reminiscent, tone, "in my young days I was very poor. . . ."

THE YEARS passed, and Joe went on, in his quiet way, making money hand over fist. I never realized how rich he was till one day, in 1940, twelve months after the outbreak of World War II, he dropped in to consult me about his health. His boys, now of an age to fight, were in uniform, and he himself was working harder than ever—building a chain of Army camps, laying out a giant transatlantic airfield.

Now, in my office, he gazed at me with friendly, tired eyes.

"Doctor," he said, "I wish you'd pep me up a little."

"What seems to be the trouble?"

"Oh, I don't know. Maybe I'm just run down. I'm depressed, worried about the future."

"What sort of worries, Joe?"

"Well, you know how everybody feels this cursed war may ruin us all, kill free enterprise, bring on inflation, shatter our economic structure. It's enough to make any man ill." His worried frown deepened. "There's Belle, you know, and the boys—I wouldn't like to see them want. I've been looking around for inflation hedges. But there just aren't any, not good ones—"

He broke off. There was a pause.

"Joe," I said suddenly, "how much are you worth?"

He gave me a shamed, sidelong glance. Then, in a low tone, he answered: "Don't tell anybody . . . but as a matter of fact, I'm worth about a million quid."

I WAS staggered. "That's a lot of money, Joe."

"Not in these days," Joe said glumly. "I might wake up tomorrow and find it wasn't worth a damn."

I gave him a thorough examination. His blood pressure was a trifle low; obviously he didn't take enough exercise; but there was nothing wrong with him—absolutely nothing to worry about. I told him so.

"Well—" Buttoning his vest, he gave me his shy, warm smile. "What are we to do about it?"

There was a very long pause.

"Joe"—I took the plunge—"why don't you try spending your money?"

"What!" He looked at me as though I were crazy. "Get rid of my capital?"

"A man carries his capital in his head nowadays. It would help you a lot, Joe—destroy a deep-buried inhibition—if you could really bring yourself to spend money, to spend it freely."

"What would I spend it on?" Joe asked.

"Oh, anything," I answered. "But especially on yourself."

I gave him a long and earnest lecture, more serious because I was on the eve of leaving for the United States to take up a post as liaison officer with the Red Cross. I hoped, most sincerely, that he would take my advice. But I felt in my heart that he would not.

I did not see him again for over nine months, and then it was in New York, where I was temporarily settled in a small apartment.

As I came up Fifth Avenue, I saw Joe standing outside an exclusive store, staring at a display of silk neckties in the window.

"Doing some shopping, Joe?" I remarked, when we had exchanged greetings. "These are very lovely ties."

"Do you know what they cost?" He paused, prepared to stun me. "Twenty-five dollars each."

"They're real silk, and hand-painted," I pointed out. "You can afford to be reckless for once. Come on, Joe. Remember what I told you."

"But twenty-five dollars for a tie!" Joe repeated in an overcome voice. "In our money, more than six pounds. Why, for that a man used to be able to get a suit of clothes, boots, socks, underwear, shirt, collar and tie—a whole outfit—and still have enough left over to pay for his dinner. Why, in my young days—"

Was it my imagination? Or did I see the gaunt figure of his aunt, muttering, muttering endlessly: "Ye can't afford it, boy!"?

I left Joe still staring into the window, still wondering, with his perplexed and worried frown, if he should buy himself a tie. Of course, I knew he wouldn't. And so I imagined it would go on until one day there would be an arresting will in the papers, with an impressive row of figures, and poor likeable old Joe, still wearing his worried frown, would be carried off in a casket, the price of which would be enough to make him turn in his grave. It was quite a sad picture, but for some reason which does me little credit, as I walked down Fifth Avenue I couldn't help myself—I burst out laughing.

Alas, I was soon to regret that stupid laughter—for my smug forecast of Joe's future had failed to envisage the tragic event which came only two months later, toward the end of October, 1941. During an air raid upon Tynecastle, a bomb fell directly upon Joe's house. Joe himself was in his office in the city, and he escaped. But his two boys, home on leave from their Army camp, were in the house, with their mother. All three were killed instantly.

I immediately sat down and wrote a long letter to Joe, full of sympathy and compunction. I received no reply—indeed, I had not expected one; I knew Joe would be completely broken up. However, about a month afterward a printed card reached me, acknowledging my condolences—the usual thing sent out in such circumstances. Apart from that, I heard nothing for at least six months.

Then, gradually, strange reports began to filter through to me. I was still domiciled in America, so that my information came infrequently and was sometimes sketchy. But I had word from several trustworthy sources, and also the evidence of certain paragraphs which kept reappearing in the Tynecastle papers.

Then I received a long letter from Sam Netley—a calm, yet glowing letter which put the matter beyond all shadow of doubt. I saw clearly that the fatal bomb which wiped out Joe's family had also blasted a lifelong complex from his soul. Yet I gasped as I stared at the list which Sam Netley had enclosed. Totaling up all contributions—the princely sums donated to bombed-out hospitals, to the Refugee Fund, and to many other organizations—I found that Joe had disbursed a full three-quarters of his fortune in charity. It was unbelievable, but it was true.

I did not see him again for nearly two years. Then, back in Tynecastle some weeks after V-E Day, I encountered Joe in the main street. I had been prepared to find a crushed and prematurely aged man. It was not so. Joe's hair had turned almost white, but he was erect, vigorous and hearty, with a smile far, far gayer than before. There was no anxiety lurking in his eyes as he clasped my hand firmly. Stripped of fear, able at last to lift his head and gaze up to the stars, he seemed like a man liberated.

Later, when we had talked long into the night, and he had told me with vast enthusiasm of his plans for a grand new Welfare Home for Tyneside children orphaned in the blitz, he gave me again that rare, new, worry-free smile. "You were right. Doctor," he said. "I never could spend my cash. But, by gum, you don't know the fun I have giving it away."

THE INNKEEPER'S WIFE

At dawn, Seraia, wife of the innkeeper, awoke, and her first instinctive glance showed that Elah, her husband, was not there beside her. She sighed and for some moments lay still, facing another day, feeling anew the weight of sadness that bore down upon her heart. She thought of the troubles in Judea, the last trace of liberty gone, the people oppressed by the harsh rule of the Roman procurator, forced to worship as idols the images of the deified Emperor set up in the temple. Throughout the land, between apathy and recklessness, a blight had spread, brigandage and robbery were rife, the taint of moral decay, of sacrilege, exaction and ill-will, hung in the air. Would nothing, she asked herself, ever come to change it? Above all, with deepening anxiety, she thought of her own difficulties, and of the painful problem which, beneath her own roof, increasingly beset her.

The morning was grey and cheerless with a harsh

breeze blowing across from Mount Hermon but, urged by her sense of duty, she stirred, got up and began to clothe herself, shivering slightly, for Bethlehem lay high on its windswept spur and the air at this season was sharp and chill. She was a comely woman still, despite her forty odd years, short and trim in figure and with an open face marked by lines of kindness. Her expression in repose showed a pleasant quietude. Her grey eyes, matching the sober hue of the robe she now girded about her, had in their depths the look of one who sees more than outward things, one who has, perhaps of necessity, created an interior life all her own.

She had finished dressing and, with a last look around the room to ensure its order, was about to leave when slowly, with a cautious touch, the door opened. It was her husband. Plainly discomfited to find her up, he hesitated irresolutely on the threshold, then, too hastily, launched into an explanation of his absence: he had gone downstairs at an early hour to prepare for the crowd of guests that must flock to the inn today; and with a sudden gust of that fretful irritability which had lately come upon him, he began to grumble at the extra work which they would have because of the great movement of people to register in the census ordained by Herod Antipas. When he paused, appearing to expect some reply, she said quietly:

"It is not like you to complain of trade, Elah."

"Of good trade, no," he retorted. "But today's may

be of a mixed variety. The rabble will be on the move."

"Then why concern yourself so deeply... you must have risen in darkness, long before the dawn?"

He reddened perceptibly under her steady gaze.

"Someone must make arrangements... yes, yes, someone must do it... so why not I...?"

While he ran on with increased confusion she answered little, pitying his weakness and shame, yet finding in these manifest emotions and in his sidelong questing glances, a faint encouragement that he still cared something for her.

As she went downstairs the light was brightening, already there were movements in the kitchen—her two good maids, Rachel and Athalea, both devoted to her, had begun the many preparations for this busy day. The cooking pots of lentils were already on the fire, water had been drawn from the well, the goat's flesh was roasting on the spit, as was proper under the Mosaic law. To Rachel, kneading the dark barley flour she had ground in the stone handmill, Seraia said:

"Today we must make an extra batch of loaves... also a special sauce of butter and milk for the meat. And fill extra gourds with olives."

"But, mistress," Rachel, the short dark one, who had a sense of humour, looked up jestingly, "if all the world is to be taxed our guests may well lack appetite."

"They will eat," Seraia said, with a faint smile, "if

only to assuage their grief." Then to Athalea: "When the bread is in the oven see that the upper rooms are made ready."

Malthace, Seraia noted with relief, had not yet appeared. She, indeed, from natural indolence, and the elaboration of her toilet, which often occupied her for an hour, or more, was always late, but her brother Zadoc was in the yard and Seraia could hear him bullying the stable boys and shouting for the wine jars to be brought in, as if he owned the place and were not a known rogue with a long record of misdemeanours who, some years before in his native Lydda, had been publicly flogged for stealing.

The rough sound of Zadoc's voice, and the thought of his sister upstairs, idly bedizening herself before her mirror, plunged a sword in Seraia's heart, but with an effort she drew herself erect and commenced her household tasks, managing in many ways through her own competence to make up for the slackness and short-tempered inefficiency which had marked her husband since Malthace and Zadoc had come to the inn, at first as servants, but soon after with a growing assertiveness and authority that could only spring from Elah's infatuation for the woman.

It was not until after the tenth hour that Malthace showed herself, announced by her loud laugh and wearing the rich, braided gown which Seraia knew Elah had given her. As she swept into the kitchen, with a look of bold effrontery and that sly air of proprietorship which cut Seraia so cruelly, she exclaimed:

"It promises right well for today There should be good pickings for us. Already there are many travellers on the road."

"Doubtless," Seraia rose from the hot roasting spit, basting spoon in hand, "but not all will be as rich or lavish as you would wish."

"Elah will single out the rich ones," the other laughed knowingly. "That I promise you."

"Then you feel that you may speak for him?" Though her nerves quivered, Seraia forced herself to answer evenly.

"Why not?" Malthace retorted, with a toss of her earrings. Placing her hands upon her hips she postured like a dancer. "Tell me, do you like my dress?"

Seraia saw her maids watching her with covert sympathy and this increased her sense of insult. But with an effort she maintained her calm and answered the servant girl.

"Yes, it is beautiful . . . and costly too, I do not doubt."

"Which makes it fitting for today. There will be excitement in plenty before we see the end of it."

Indeed, as Malthace had said, there presently began a great stir without and a great commotion within. Situated as it was, among the olive groves on the main road to Bethlehem—which lay, girded and fortified by the great wall of Rehoboam, a bare quarter of a league away—the inn was passed by all the traffic to and from the town. Founded by Elah's grandfather, a man of high integrity and a member of the council of the Zealots, of whom it was said he would rather lose ten talents than overcharge one shekel, the hostel had in these days enjoyed a high and sober reputation. Now, in Elah's hands, this was less than formerly, but he had made extensions, adding a large atrium, lit from above, in the Roman manner, and with this and other modern innovations, still commanded an abundant though perhaps a less exclusive patronage.

Thus before the day was far advanced the place was filled to overflowing, all rooms occupied or bespoken, the long atrium packed with a noisy throng, eating and drinking, some disputing violently, others forgetting the discomforts of their enforced journey and the gloomy prospect of the new Roman taxes by making merry.

Amongst them Elah bustled officiously, scolding the kitchen maids, interfering with the waiters, but always with a sharp eye to the main chance—it seemed to Seraia that his love of gain, grown within recent months, had never been more evident. Nor had Malthace and Zadoc ever seemed nearer to him, always at his elbow, smiling, prompting, propitiating, yet with an interchange of glances between themselves that, to Seraia, boded ill.

Indeed, for the innkeeper's wife, as the oppressive noontide passed and the long, noisy afternoon wore on, a strange sense of personal crisis began to form and take shape within her. What, she asked herself, would be the outcome of it all? She believed that Elah still respected her, yet he seemed more and more under the domination of Malthace. After twenty years of marriage she knew her husband, knew him to be wellmeaning in many ways, soft by nature rather than severe, a man absorbed by commerce who, despite his uncertainty of temper, had on the whole been considerate towards her in the past. But lately he had changed and, obsessed with those material things which to her were of slight importance, had fallen into that self-indulgence spread by the loose ideas and looser living of the Imperial masters.

Of one thing she felt sure—if only their child had lived this would not have happened ... yes, that would have bound them together. But it had been the will of the Almighty to take their son and now, with that tie unloosed, with nothing to restrain him, of what might not Elah be capable? Might he not even put her away? She trembled at the thought which had long tormented her. He would not be the first who had cast off his lawful wife and taken the bondwoman to his bed. She had prayed that it might not be, yet such things were commonplace in these evil days when immorality was rife and paganism swept the land.

It was just then, towards the fifth hour, that Seraia, meditating thus as she helped her maids scour the piles of platters borne in from the dining hall, suddenly heard her husband's voice raised angrily in the yard. Looking out she saw that a man, advanced in years, and a young woman, dusty and travel-stained, had come to the back door of the inn.

"I tell you we have no room," Elah's tone rose higher. "You must go elsewhere."

"But, sir," entreated the old man, "we have sought everywhere in Bethlehem and there also not a single lodging is to be found."

Seraia drew nearer the open window, wiping her hands upon her apron, observing the drawn look of endurance on the young woman's face and the weariness of her companion as he leaned upon his staff. Now, humbly, and in a deeply troubled voice he was again begging Elah to reconsider his refusal. They had come far, he pleaded; his name, he added, with touching simplicity, was Joseph, and Mary, his young wife, was even now expecting to be delivered of her firstborn. Only the edict of the procurator Herod had forced them to journey at such a time—in this extremity they must have shelter of some kind.

"Of your goodness," he concluded, "could you not spare us a corner beneath your roof?"

"I have not even a garret," Elah almost shouted. "Can you not understand, the inn is full? And were it not, there would still be no room for such as you."

As the innkeeper turned away, the rejected travellers stood in silence: Mary with downcast eyes, her husband so bowed in troubled perplexity it was plain he knew not what to do. Meanwhile Zadoc and one of the waiters, standing by, found the opportunity to demonstrate their wit too good to miss.

"Ay, ay, this is a sorry pass you're in," Zadoc began, with affected concern. "Had we known of your distinguished coming we should certainly have reserved our finest chamber . . . plenished it with brocades from Damascus, rich carpets from Persia, furnishings of sandalwood inlaid with ivory and mother-of-pearl. . . ." His grin broke through and, encouraged by the sniggers of his ally, leaning idly against the wall, he continued to mock the two wayfarers.

To these jeers Joseph made no answer but, taking Mary's arm, slowly turned away. Touched in her generous heart, Seraia could bear it no longer. She must not, could not, let them go. Impulsively she ran from the kitchen and caught the dusty sleeve of Mary's dress. Because of Elah she dared not take them into the house. Perhaps he was watching even now, ready to forbid and rebuke her. Hurriedly, she conducted them across the yard towards the low straggle of outbuildings on the opposite side and, pushing open an unlatched door, drew them into the protective darkness of the stable. This was no more than a deep recess cut from the ridge of red volcanic earth that marked the boundary of the courtyard, but it was faced with sun-dried bricks and thatched with stout osiers. At the back, dimly seen, an ox and a young ass lay together in their stall.

"It is poor enough, the Lord knows," Seraia said, breathing a little quickly from nervousness and haste, "but it is all I have to offer. Still . . . here at least is shelter, warmth against the keen wind, and a clean litter of straw on which to rest."

"We are grateful... most grateful," Joseph said, gazing at her earnestly. "Heaven will bless you for your kindness."

"You will not mind the animals?" Seraia ventured, with anxious solicitude. "They are quiet beasts."

"We are country people... we shall be at home with them," Joseph answered. Then turning to Mary he pressed her hand, murmuring reassuringly: "Be of good cheer. It is come to pass... exactly as in my dream."

These strange words, though spoken in an undertone, were heard distinctly by the innkeeper's wife. They surprised and confounded her. So too did the calm and inevitable air with which the travellers accepted this makeshift haven in which they found themselves. Hurriedly, almost with embarrassment, she said:

"I will bring you some refreshment." And, even as Joseph started to thank her, she hastened away. It was not easy to procure the food under her husband's watchful eye, but here again she was successful and in no more than a few minutes had returned, bringing barley bread, slices of goat's cheese, and a brimming bowl of milk. Nor was her intervention too soon. Both were faint for want of sustenance but beyond this she saw that Mary, worn to the point of collapse, was already suffering in silence the pangs of labour. And so, with deepening compassion, the innkeeper's wife set out to help her.

Afternoon turned to evening with a sky from

which the clouds had passed, leaving the heavens bathed in a strange pellucid twilight, and Seraia, between her duties at the inn, made many journeys across the courtyard. By taking her good maid, Rachel, into her confidence, thus far she had succeeded in accomplishing all these missions unobserved—an augury bringing much relief, for now she stood so deeply committed she dreaded discovery by Elah. Yet, come what may, she must go on. Begun in charity, this work of human kindness insensibly had assumed for her a different character, mysterious and momentous, even intimidating. These were no ordinary vagrants. Joseph, when questioned, revealed that he came of the house of David—a royal line. Advanced so far in years beyond his youthful bride, withal so gentle, he appeared more a guardian than a husband. And Mary, over and above her modesty and beauty, possessed a dignity striking in one so young. In the uncomplaining serenity with which she submitted to the humble circumstances of her confinement, it seemed almost as though she knew these to be predestined. This sky, too, windless now, and of an unearthly purity, in which a great star had suddenly appeared, distant yet brilliant, increased Seraia's sense of fearful wonderment. She asked herself if she was not partaking in some great event, she knew not what, and at this a sweet thought came to her. On an impulse to give what was dearest to her heart she climbed to the attic of the inn. Here, under the roof tree, laid carefully away in a cedar chest were the swaddling clothes which, ten years before, she had made with loving fingers, for her own child. Between pain and tenderness Seraia viewed them, breathing the fragrance of the cedarwood, reflecting wistfully on her own loss, on all that might have been, and on the strange undreamed-of use to which now, with gladness, she would put these soft, long-treasured garments. Swiftly she took them up.

But as she came down, bearing them, all expectant of the joy of giving, she drew up short. There, at the foot of the stairs, Elah was awaiting her, his look charged with anger and resentment. In the shadows of the passage Malthace was visible behind him.

"What's this you are about, woman?" he burst forth. "Did I not send these two beggars upon their way? Yet I am told you have given them both food and shelter. And now," he bent forward, outraged, pulling at the clothes, "these."

She had turned pale, realizing that the woman had spied, then informed, upon her. But she answered bravely, in a tone mingling resolution with entreaty.

"Their need is great, Elah; how could I do otherwise than help them? I beg you not to interfere. There is in this . . . something beyond our understanding."

"Beyond whose understanding?" he cried.

"Have you not seen the great star . . . rising . . . there in the East? It is a sign, Elah."

"What nonsense are you talking? Once and for all, I forbid you to continue this . . . this . . . wasteful folly."

A moment of silence, prolonged and absolute, while with downcast eyes Seraia sustained the gaze of her husband and Malthace. Then she raised her head and faced him steadily.

"No, Elah, I must do it."

Quite taken aback, he stood gaping—but only for an instant.

"What . . . would you openly disobey me?" And in an access of violence he raised his hand and struck her on the face.

The force and unexpectedness of the blow drove Seraia back. Yet she did not fall and, with a sharp intake of breath, recovered herself. With bent head and without a word she hurried off towards the yard.

"You see," Malthace murmured, coming nearer, "how little she respects you. Are you not the master here? Why should you be browbeaten by her when there are others who would bend to your slightest wish?" And she leaned enticingly against him.

But for once, Elah did not respond. Bitter though he was against Seraia, he was now, by a swift turn of mood, equally angry with himself. It seemed impossible that he had struck her. Never before had he used violence against her. The thing was unaccountable. Yet surely she had merited it. Advancing to the doorway he watched the retreating figure of his wife who, for the first time in her life, had disregarded his authority. Why had she done so? And what was the meaning of the strange words she had used? It was at this moment that, looking up involuntarily towards the sky, he perceived the star which though far away, actually seemed to move toward the inn. Glittering in the tremulous twilight, a scintilla of brilliance, it caught and held him motionless, until abruptly he drew away his gaze. Disturbed and undecided, he turned restlessly towards Malthace.

"Let us go in and drink a cup of wine," he said. "I am sick to death of this talk of signs and portents."

They went to the cabinet opening from the vestibule which he used as his office and there, from a cool jar, holding the sweet vintage which, because she favoured it, he had specially obtained from Petra, he poured two generous measures. It was a habit he had fallen into and which at first had highly entertained him—snatching a respite from the humdrum round in amorous dalliance, amused by her idle chatter and the blandishments she freely exercised upon him. But now here was little pleasure in it. Somehow the wine did not refresh him, nor did the woman's flattery ease his sullen mood. He remained dull and silent and after a brief interlude he rose and went into the atrium. Here were gathered most of the guests, now returned from the registration booths and awaiting the evening meal. Mingling with them, Elah felt more himself, assumed the business of a host, joining in the general conversation, discussing the census and the Roman levy which must follow it. In this serious talk of money and imposts, no mention was made of anything so trivial and unremunerative as the star. Yet an hour later when Elah emerged, more comfortable in mind, there was Seraia, waiting in the passage for him, recalling the whole disconcerting affair by her rapt exclamation:

"The child is born!"

Her face was bright, her look almost radiant, the blow he had given her seemed banished from her recollection, for all in that one communicative breath she added:

"And I . . . I held him in my arms."

"Well, what of it?" he said roughly, withdrawing from the hand she would have laid upon his arm. "All has been done against my will."

"But hear me, Elah," she eagerly persisted, undeterred by the rebuff. "There was of course no place for him. Can you fancy what I did . . . took fresh straw, made a little bed and laid him in it . . . in the manger. At first the ox was startled, then came forward and licked his little foot. Come, Elah, come and see for yourself. I entreat you. It is a sight you must not miss."

"Let me be." He shook her off. "I will have no part of it. There is no reason in what you say."

"I cannot speak of reason, or of what manner of child this may be . . . only this . . . when I held him in my arms it was as though my heart thrilled and sang within me."

Part of him wanted to respond in unwilling recognition of her goodness but his other self choked back the inclination. Because of this inner struggle, because he blamed her as the cause of it, he sought the harder for words with which to hurt her.

"What a fool you are," he said, "to drivel thus over an unknown brat. And a shrewish fool besides ... striving to press your will upon me. Go now and see about the serving of the supper."

When she had gone, he felt appeased by her submission, once again master of his household. Yet this reversal of his mood did not last, for presently that provoking and unnatural malaise began, once more, to harass him. He could not shake it off, and against his will, drawn irresistibly, he found himself, by a roundabout way, back in the courtyard, gazing upwards uneasily out of the corner of his eye. Yes, the star was still there, and still drawing nearer, larger and more luminous than before. Could it be, in truth, a portent? As he struggled with the question, suddenly, to his surprise, he saw some shepherds from the neighboring fields approaching the inn. They had no business here at this hour yet on they came, in their shaggy wool cloaks and thonged leggings, a band of seven or eight, led by old Joab, who was piping the little tune with which he homed his flock. Old Joab was a queer one, judged wise by some and simple by others, a man who knew herbs and their uses, foretold the weather, studied the heavens, and even explained dreams. A solitary who lived alone, tending his sheep and seeking no man's company, there were many nonetheless who sought his, for he could heal the sick and, it was whispered, make predictions which came true. When asked about such powers he would reply that he had no powers, but that sometimes in the wide spaces of the wilderness he heard voices—which stamped him, of course, in the eyes of the learned, as a natural half-wit.

Now, when Elah called to him, asking the reason of his coming, he finished first his little tune, then gaily gave back these preposterous words:

"We are come, master, to give honour to the new-born Babe."

"Honour, you old clown?" the innkeeper shouted back. "Are you out of your mind?"

"If so, it's for joy, master. This is a day that has long been waited for, and one that will be long remembered."

And forthwith he grouped his band about the stable and, with a preliminary flourish, led them in what, despite the untutored voices and the feeble tootling of the pipe, was plainly intended as a canticle of praise and jubilation.

Biting his lip, Elah stood watching and listening in acute vexation. It was beyond his comprehension, this unlooked for performance, and so also was the whole sequence of events which had been, as it were, arranged and enacted on the very threshold of his inn.

For some woman of no account to bear her child obscurely when on a journey, that surely was commonplace. Why then had his wife lost her wits in a passion of devotion, why had these idiot carollers been drawn from their fields to stand moping and mowing to a reedy tune? Why, above all, this unique, incredible star? With all his soul Elah wanted to cross the yard, his own yard, throw open the stable door, his own door, and pierce the very core of the conundrum. He could not do it: stubbornness, pride, and something else—a vague fear of the unknown, of what to his own undoing he might discover—all this held him back. Instead, he swung round and reentered his inn. As he did so he almost stumbled over the figure of Zadoc sunk down in a dark corner of the passage, befuddled with wine, and snoring noisily. The sight, though it was no novelty, depressed Elah further. He touched the sot with his foot but failed to rouse him; then, after a moment of gloomy contemplation, he went into his office, began to prepare the reckonings for the morrow.

When he finished, supper had finally been served; indeed, was almost over. Moodily watching the last dishes being cleared, Elah realized that it was time for him to go to register. As one of the most important men in the district and a close friend of Ammon the publican who, besides occupying the position of local tax collector, was now acting as the chief census teller, Elah had no need to scramble with the common herd but could go privately after the official hours. Ammon indeed owed him many favours: a bag of flour here—a cask of wine there, delivered from the inn after dark, had created a solid understanding between them, and Elah well knew from his experience in the past that he would receive a highly favourable treatment under the new tax levy.

The prospect of this visit and, even more, the thought of quitting the inn came to him with relief. He was soon ready and as he set off into Bethlehem he hoped that the change of scene, together with the movement of his limbs, might lift the cloud that hung upon him. But it was not so. The faster and the farther he went, the more spiritless his thoughts became. In the town, adding to his oppression, he found that the star-struck shepherds had gone before him, still in an exalted state, and were even now parading the streets, singing their crazy hymns, proclaiming tidings of great joy for all people, crying aloud that light has come into the world, that the glory of the Lord was around them.

Avoiding these madmen, Elah spent an hour in close and confidential communion with Ammon, then he called on another acquaintance, ordered some stores to be delivered next day, but all the while he was not himself; there was no relish in his bargaining, nor in his most profitable meeting with the publican.

When he got back to the inn the windows were darkened, the hubbub of the long day was stilled. Now perhaps he might find some peace. But when he threw himself upon his bed, his sleep was fitful and disturbed. He rose unrefreshed and met the morning with a sullen frown. Indeed, all that day, and during the days that followed, there lay upon the innkeeper a fearful indecision. Though now he made no move to interfere, covertly, with a brooding disquiet, he watched the comings and goings of his wife in her ministrations to the mother and the child. And all the time the great star drew nearer. He felt he could endure it no longer. Then, late one night, as he took his keys and went the rounds of his establishment, preparing to lock up, a sudden sound of hooves made him spin round. Three horsemen, richly dressed and of dark complexion were entering the courtyard, urging their mounts to a canter, as though at long last they saw their destination before them. Expert from long experience in appraising the social order, Elah perceived at once that these were men of the highest rank, perhaps even—from the jewels they wore, their swinging scimitars and richly hued turbans— potentates from the East. Instinctively, as they drew up, habit and the thought of gain drove him forward, bowing and scraping, servilely offering hospitality.

"Welcome, good sirs... your excellencies. You have ridden far, I see. Permit me to take your horses. You shall have the best my house can offer."

Did they understand him? Did they even hear him? To his chagrin they ignored him—a passing glance, calm and detached, was all that he received. Then, one said, with an air of high authority, but using the words awkwardly and with a foreign accent:

"We do not stay. Only see that no one disturbs us while we are here."

Dismounting, they unstrapped their saddlebags and shook the dust from their garments; then, as Elah stood, mortified and dumbfounded, they looked upwards towards the star which now was stationary, shining directly above them, spoke a few words in low tones amongst themselves, and entered the stable.

Now, indeed, the innkeeper could hold back no longer. A fearful curiosity bore down his stubborn resistance, overcame his fear of discovering, in the unknown, something which of its very nature would hurt and humiliate him. Slowly, step by step, as though drawn by some unseen and irresistible force, he followed the three strangers and, taking his stance at the half-open doorway, peered within.

The interior was dim, lit only by a shallow vessel of oil in which a wick of plaited rushes flickered, casting soft shadows into the corners of the cave and amongst the bare beams which held the osier roof. Yet the scene was plainly visible, vivid and distinct, as though limned by the brush of some great master. Mary, the mother, reclining upon a pallet of straw, held the Child closely in her arms, while Joseph, having risen to greet the visitors, now stood back, withdrawn, shrouded in his grey cloak. Behind, the ox and the ass lay peacefully in the dimness of their stall. All this Elah might have anticipated, though he could not have foreseen its simplicity and beauty. What struck and stupefied him was the behaviour of the three men of rank, these rich and powerful rulers from the East. There, with his own eyes, he observed them step forward, each in his turn, kneel reverently on the earthen floor and offer homage to the newborn Child; then, having made obeisance, each humbly proffered a gift. Craning forward, Elah caught his breath as he discerned the rare nature of the offerings—myrrh, frankincense, and gold. All these Mary, the mother, received in silence, simply, timidly, and with a kind of awe, as though submissive to a ritual not yet perhaps fully understood but for which in her heart she knew herself predestined. The Babe, resting close against her breast, also seemed conscious of the ceremony enacted before Him, for His gaze, lingering upon the three visitants, followed their movements with a strange and touching solemnity.

All this, to the innkeeper, so passed comprehension he began to question its reality, striking his forehead with his knuckles as though to dispel a mirage of self-delusion. Was he drunk or was he dreaming? A beggar child, chance begotten in this stable, venerated, yes, worshipped, by three high-born kings. He could not as a rational man find reason in it. Ah yes, he clung to the phrase . . . a rational man . . . like a swimmer in deep water overcome and reaching for support. Was he not practical, sensible and shrewd, a realist steeped in sound logic, a man of the world whose skeptical eye had many times pierced a bogus scheme or a concocted story? It was madness to shout of glory and great joy, of a light to lighten the world, when some sane material reason must exist, and would be found, to explain this mummery.

But suddenly, as he rejected all the mystery of this mysterious event, the songs of the shepherds, the visitation of the kings and the portent of the star, the child in his mother's arms moved slightly and turned its gaze full upon him. As that single glance from those innocent and unreproachful eyes, filled with such tenderness and grace, fell upon the innkeeper, he could not sustain it. A shock passed through him; his own glance fell to the ground. Instinctively he turned away and, like one intent only upon escape, went back across the yard as though pursued.

The inn was quiet now, servants and guests alike had retired for the night. But in an anteroom, as Elah entered, one light remained unextinguished and there, seated alone, was Malthace. She wore a loose robe, ungirded; her cheek was flushed from some hot and pungent brew and her dark hair, unbound, fell across her shoulders. The smile with which she greeted him was warm with invitation.

"Where have you been? I had begun to fear you would not come. And after such a day when I have had but the barest word with you." She stretched her arm towards him. "Come, sit and drink with me. Tell me I am kind to wait for you. Then speak to me of love."

Dazed by the light, the unexpected sight of her and above all by the turmoil of his thoughts, Elah passed one hand across his eyes and with the other supported himself against the lintel of the door.

"Why? Are you not well?" Then she laughed meaningly. "Is it the need of me that turns you so weak?"

He did not answer. She was the last person he had wished to see. In the revulsion of his feelings she was at this moment repugnant to him. But he dared not, from very shame, expose his weakness to her.

"I am tired perhaps," he muttered. "As you say . . . the day has been long."

"Then come sit by me and I will refresh you." She repeated her gesture of invitation.

"No. . . ." With head averted, he fumbled for an excuse. "I am indeed weary, Malthace . . . there was much for me to do . . . tonight I must rest."

Her face changed, hardened—less at the words than at the manner of his refusal.

"Come now, Elah," she cried sharply, "you cannot treat me thus. . . ."

But before she could protest further, he turned and went away.

In truth, a great lassitude had come upon him and, heavily, as though each foot were weighted with lead, he climbed the steep stairs to his room. He had thought to find his wife asleep but despite the lateness of the hour she had not yet retired. Seated on a low stool by the open window, a pensive, lonely figure lined against the brightness of the heavens, she was gazing outwards, so still and self-absorbed she seemed unaware that he had entered. Something in her posture, or in his own state of mind, arrested him and, though he wished to speak, left him at a loss for words. And suddenly he felt drawn to her, with an acuteness of emotion he had not experienced for years, not since those early days when, as an awkward youth, he had sought her in marriage. In the present confusion of his thoughts he longed to converse with her, to open his heart and confide in her. But that was an intimacy he had lost during these past months and awareness that the fault was his left him constrained and mute. Yet he had to speak; it was a necessity that could not be denied, and finally, with an effort, he broke the silence.

"Is it not time you were abed? You have worked hard these past days."

"They have not seemed hard," she replied, without moving. "For me this has been a time of gladness."

"Then do not mar it with a fever. You know the night air suits you ill. Draw the shutter and I will light the lamp."

"Need you?" she queried, in a low voice. "Is not there light enough from the star without?"

"Ay, the star," he answered and broke off. Then, not to expose himself, he tried feebly to introduce a touch of lightness to his tone. "Odd things have happened here of late . . . and tonight as well. As I went to lock up, three purse-proud strangers appeared . . . a haughty trio, I warrant you . . . they would have none of us. What business they were about I could not tell."

"They have gone," she said quietly. "I saw them come and I saw them take their leave only a moment ago, so doubtless they have accomplished what they came for."

He saw that she was looking down towards the row of outbuildings now wrapped in perfect stillness, and more than ever he felt within him the pressing need to reveal his state of mind, and to seek in her wise experience an elucidation of his incredible enigma which from first to last had so unceasingly afflicted him. But before he could grasp it, the moment passed—with a sigh she had risen and begun to shade the window, saying:

"I had better shut out the brightness Otherwise you will not sleep."

In silence they began to disrobe and presently they had composed themselves to rest. But weary as he was, and try as he would, Elah could not find the respite of sleep which he craved. Never had he known such affliction of mind, such abject desolation of soul, such a crushing sense of his own worthlessness. It was as though for the first time he saw himself with the eyes of truth. The foundations on which he had built his life, the whole comfortable structure of his existence, had been undermined by the sequence of events which had marked these past days. In this moment of enlightenment and self-revelation all that he had sought and striven for so avidly—profit and gain, worldly success, the pleasures of the senses—all now seemed futile and sordid. Especially did he perceive in its true light the folly and danger of his involvement with Malthace. He had never loved her. It was a mere infatuation, surrender to flattery and enticement by a man past his prime.

And then, by contrast, his thoughts turned to Seraia, his wife, who for so many years had made life's journey with him, worked by his side, endured his irritable words, his moods and selfishness, suffered without complaint, the heat and burden of the day. How could he have taken all this for granted, without a word of gratitude? Patience and kindness, regard for her neighbor, the desire to do good, above all a constant unselfishness—these were her qualities, all hitherto unacknowledged, and they rose to confront and accuse him. A dampness broke upon his brow. That unearthly light, penetrating the slats of the shutter, cast bars of shadow on the walls, seemed to imprison him in his iniquity. Swept by a wave of compunction and remorse he turned to her.

"Seraia . . . are you awake?"

She answered him at once: she, too, had been unable to sleep. A tense silence vibrated between them, then, at last, the strings of his tongue were loosed. In a broken voice, with a rush of words that told of his troubled spirit, he acknowledged his unfaithfulness, expressed his sorrow, asked her forgiveness. He would break with Malthace, send her away, with her brother, tomorrow. She heard him in silence, holding his hand with a consoling touch, and when he ceased she soothed him with calm and tender words.

After this release of all that had been upon his mind, a great relief came to him. It was like a burden thrown off and, with renewed intimacy, he began to talk freely, confidingly, even in some degree extravagantly, since this was precisely his nature, that in his rebound from the depths he should soar to the opposite extreme.

"Tell me, Seraia . . . dear wife . . . all that has occurred . . . what do you make of it?"

"I do not know. But of one thing I am sure. There is a heavenly secret in what we have witnessed here."

"For my part," he meditated, "striving to put the facts together—and you know I have always been a logical man—this little one could well be the son of someone most important—an august personage . . . the Lord alone knows whom . . . yet one who for his own good reasons might wish at this stage to conceal the child's origin. All the circumstances, especially the obscurity of the birth—though the meaning of this is not altogether clear to me—seem in great measure to support this view." He ran on like this for a few minutes, extemporizing, then concluded fulsomely: "Be that as it may, I will admit freely that I regret my unfeeling conduct in the matter—so much indeed, that I would willingly make reparation."

The innkeeper paused. Ever since the Child's glance had struck into his heart, a longing had germinated there, born of an unsuspected love and fostered by the instinct of possession. Thus with a touch of his old self-importance he resumed:

"I have been thinking, dear wife . . . if perhaps . . . we might offer to take the infant for our own."

For a moment she did not reply. Then she shook her head slowly, but with certainty.

"No, Elah, that could never be. What mother would give up such a one?"

"But consider the advantages we could offer. We are well off . . . at least," he interpolated cautiously, "moderately so . . . I could well afford to be generous and kind."

There was a brief silence then, seriously, she said:

"This very afternoon I spoke with Joseph. He told me they must leave tomorrow."

"Tomorrow!" Elah exclaimed. "It is not possible."

"Yes, it is possible. The mother is young and strong. And if danger threatens her child she will not tarry."

"Danger?"

"Herod, the procurator, means evil towards the little one."

"Ah, come, my good wife; I think you carry it somewhat too far. What proof have you of this? Did Joseph say from whom the warning came?"

"There are some, Elah . . . a chosen few . . . who are not guided by the voices of the world. Such were the prophets . . . and such . . . though he does not prophesy, is this good man. I assure you they must leave us, and for a while go afar from here."

He made as if to speak, then restrained himself. Holding to his own opinion, he nevertheless did not wish to contradict her, to oppress her with argument or reassert his will. His feeling towards her was too sweet, his assuagement too complete. He merely said, with what for him was unaccustomed mildness:

"Tomorrow I will rise up betimes. I will speak to your worthy Joseph, reason with him kindly, persuade him . . . you will see."

She realized that he had caught only a glimmer of what, so clearly for her, was a celestial light, that while he marveled at the mystery, still could view it only on a natural plane. Yet in the happiness of her reconciliation she was content to hold her peace. And in peace they fell asleep.

But indeed, when morning came Elah, the first to awake, remained intent upon his purpose. He roused Seraia, bade her dress quickly and come with him downstairs. She smiled at his tone of urgency but made it her pleasure to humour him. Avoiding the kitchen, where the maids were already stirring, they went by the side passage to the back premises. The sun was rising and the walls and the roofs of Bethlehem, outlined against the dappled sky, were caught by the blush of dawn. The air struck cool and fresh, and already wild doves were circling above the olive groves which lay on the slopes beyond. Elah had taken his wife by the arm as they made their way across the courtyard. Although she knew in advance what they must find, Seraia, hoping against hope, could feel her heart beating painfully as Elah knocked, then threw open the stable door.

Yes, they had gone. Except for the ox and the ass, the little hut was empty. Slowly the innkeeper entered, followed by his wife, glancing around in his disappointment, as though searching for something, a trace of its occupants, that might still remain. The place had been neatly tidied, the floor cleared of straw and carefully swept, everything indeed restored to an carefully swept, everything indeed restored to an order better than before. In the air there faintly lingered the mingled aromatic odours of myrrh and frankincense and, on the edge of the manger where the Child had lain, there had been left a piece of gold.

"You see," Seraia could not resist the quiet rebuke, "Mary has made payment for her lodging."

Elah coloured deeply: the gold indeed would have settled tenfold the reckoning for his best room. He picked up the precious metal, which was not a coin but an oddly fashioned piece, bearing still, no doubt, the shape in which it had come from the mine or from some distant riverbed. For a long moment he studied it in silence then, strange in one usually so covetous, he handed it to his wife.

"Take it . . . it is yours."

Seraia took the piece. She, too, noted with surprise its singular outline. It had the rough form of a cross.

"And now," Elah braced himself, "there is much for me to do. I pray you leave me till it is done." With his head erect he swung round and went before her towards the inn.

Back in her room Seraia stood for a while in anxious speculation. Would Elah carry through his resolution to send Malthace and her brother away? How often in the past had he expressed his good intentions and failed in the end to carry them out. She knew his inconstant nature, knew too that such weakness was not cured overnight. Yet this time she was hopeful, yes, she fully believed that his effort to redeem himself would succeed. A wave of happiness surged over her. Mindful of a fine filigree chain which at her betrothal, years before, Elah had given her, she sought it, found it finally in a forgotten casket laid away in a drawer. Then, threading her little cross upon the chain, she placed it around her neck.

The ordinary day of the inn was beginning—the cooking pots bubbling in the kitchen, guests moving in the passages, shouting and clattering over the cobblestones of the courtyard. Had these days of wonder ever been? All might have seemed a dream but for the cross that lay upon her breast. Yet for Seraia it was no dream. In her mind's eye she saw the little family moving bravely on . . . Mary, Joseph, and the Child . . . ever advancing on their predetermined path, suffering hardship and persecution, fulfilling their heavenly destiny. Tears moistened her eyes as she remembered the indescribable happiness of holding the Babe in her arms. He shall be great, she thought . . . and it was I who saw and held Him on the day that He was born. Would others, now or in the future, ever feel the sweetness of that blessed day? She could not tell but, fingering the cross, she vowed: every year, as long as I live, though I am the only one in all the world to do so, I shall keep the birthday of this Child, and keeping it, I shall know happiness. Then, softly to herself, as though treasuring it, she murmured that name which Mary had told her they would give Him.

LILY OF THE VALLEY

GILBERT LENNARD was a sick man when he came off the boat that gray spring day, yet his vanity carried him through the stir, the inevitable sensation of his arrival. He faced the ring of reporters and cameramen with his usual sophisticated boredom, supplied some patronizing information as to his immediate movements, then left for his hotel suite with his Japanese valet and Jones, his English secretary.

Lennard had crossed from London for the gala performance of his *Manhattan Moonshine,* a smash hit on Broadway for the past year, and afterwards he had it in mind to fly to the Coast to supervise the final arrangements for the film production of his *Spanish Highway.* But whatever he did, or meant to do, Lennard was always a front-page splash. His fame as a playwright. composer and producer, long escaped from the familiar aspersions of precocious brilliance, had reached the international zenith. It was no uncommon occurrence to find a Lennard play drawing the town simultaneously in London, New York and Paris.

He had an uncanny finger for the public pulse. a flair for anticipation, and his versatility fell little short of genius. He succeeded with everything, from straight drama to light comedy. His operetta, *Perdiia,* had been rated by serious critics as fit to rank with Gilbert and Sullivan. Since he had been on the stage in his early days, he frequently took the lead in his own plays. He had broken into the movies with brilliant success, swelling his income, already enormous, to a staggering figure.

And beyond all this, he was young—not more than thirty-five—smart, cynical, dissolute and superlatively the vogue. In an orbit which swung from Mayfair to Miami he moved in that exclusive international society where the race is only to the swift. His success with women was said to be amazing. He was, in short, a celebrity of the first magnitude.

On the present night of his arrival in New York there was a party in Lennard's apartment. Fifty floors above the lights of Park Avenue, to the long green-and-gold room decorated in the style *Chinois,* a mob of people, famous and infamous, had gravitated by a kind of unnatural law, to see and be seen. Lennard, of course—Lennard in his brocade dressing gown, cigaret in the celebrated elongated holder—was holding the center of the floor, his lined face sardonic. his eyes weary and slightly sneering. He had been keeping himself up with brandy and was now somberly drunk. entertaining his audience by the satiric, unsmiling brilliance of his wit.

Seen closely, he was not in the least good-looking—he was too spare, dark and sallow. His tallness, combined with the angularity of his shoulders, gave him a gaunt and burnt-out look. His cheeks were deeply lined, his cheekbones prominent, and the curve of his mouth was both bitter and sad. But he had strange and fascinating charm.

As usual, he was dramatizing himself, deliberately occupying the spotlight. Nevertheless, it was easy to understand why women found him irresistible. He was quite unscrupulous, his outlook so disillusioned it had fixed him in an attitude of utter cynicism. He took everything and gave nothing. He liked to call himself a realist. And tonight, as he gazed around, he decided with a bitter smile that, despite the flattery and adulation which surrounded him, he had not one genuine friend in the world.

The party ground itself out at last. And if Lennard had been a sick man before, on the morning afterwards he felt definitely worse. He had slept badly and there was a ridiculous stitch in his side which kept at him, like a nagging wife. But with characteristic perversity he struggled into a bathrobe about eleven-thirty for coffee and an irritable survey of the Sunday newspapers.

Later, his secretary came in. Lennard kept the man standing a long time before he deigned to notice him—it was a trick he employed with all his servants.

"What am I doing today?"

"Lunching at Jonstown, Long Island, sir."

An unpleasant pause.

"Rather important, sir," Jones conciliated, with one eye on the book and the other on the jaded face before him. "You promised Mr. Day you'd run down to discuss the new Vestris contract."

"I remember." Lennard muttered, pressing his head against his hand. "But not for lunch. I couldn't stand it. Ring up Day and tell him I can't come. No, stop, it may do me good to get out of this damned apartment for a bit. Tell him I'll be down by three. But first of all, get Taki to fix me a highball. I feel like the visible personification of death."

Toward three o'clock, fortified by a fair quantity of Scotch, Lennard drove down to the Day home on Long Island. It was a quiet April afternoon, and as the black-and-silver roadster crossed the East River, passed through the outlying suburbs, then swished down the cold concrete speedway between fields and woodlands not yet wakened from their winter apathy, Lennard felt a curious lassitude steal over him.

He hardly knew Sam Day, vice president of the Vestris Picture Corporation, remembering him vaguely as a short, bulky, distressingly ordinary American businessman. He resigned himself to the customary display of Vestris magnificence, to vulgarly ostentatious hospitality and a flattering inveiglement toward the two-hundred-thousand-dollar contract with which the corporation was enticing him. Already he felt his gorge rise; he blamed himself for coming.

But Jonstown, when he reached it, occasioned him a mild surprise. The place was not fashionable, and not at all large—a plain white colonial house, old and simple, with severe unpillared portico set away from the road among natural and unspoiled surroundings. As they turned up the drive he had an impression of a plantation of pines, a wide shimmering lake with its outlet in a swift millrace; then the car crunched to rest on the gravel forecourt, and somehow he was out and in the hall, being heartily pump-handled by Day himself.

"Glad to see you. Mr. Lennard, sir." Sam beamed all over his genial face. He was florid and baldish. "We were awfully sorry you couldn't make it for lunch. But now you're here—well, that's the main thing. Yes, sir. Come right in and meet Mrs. Sam."

Lennard grimaced. Day's laugh vibrated through his head like a pneumatic drill, and the stitch which had troubled him all morning began to grip him distressingly with every breath. Reluctantly he followed his host into the drawing-room.

"Well, now, Ma. This is Mr. Lennard. I guess you've heard of him. And then some!" A boyish grin, displaying much gold, was accompanied by an expansive hand-wave. "Mr. Lennard, meet my wife."

At the barbarous introduction a faint shudder passed over Lennard. He advanced frigidly toward the woman who sat by the long French window, her face half in shadow, her figure outlined against the afternoon light, Though he barely glanced at her as she smiled without moving from her chair, he saw she was neither young nor remarkable. Yet for some reason she roused in him a violent antipathy.

The conversation, sustained mainly by the voluble Sam, ran for a moment on depressingly conventional lines. Then, with a shy gesture. the woman turned.

"You look tired, Mr. Lennard. Will you let me give you some tea?"

He stared over her head with more than his usual rudeness. "No, thank you. I'm not an addict of the muslin bag."

She smiled slightly. "But neither are we. Will you have Indian or China?"

Her suburban amiability, and the failure of his offensive manner to disturb it, heightened Lennard's exasperation. The simplicity of her gray dress, the careless, out-of-fashion mode in which her hair was done, a quality of repose which pervaded her body, all had their innocent part in this incitement—but it was her eyes which most acutely provoked him. They were of a light hazel, steady, direct, and so frankly unsophisticated—virginal was the word he sneeringly applied—that they outraged the first principles of his experience.

Moodily he sat and watched her as she dealt with the tea equipage which a maidservant brought in. He noticed that her fingernails were unstained by lacquer. She wore no makeup, no lip rouge. Her teeth were white and even. There were tiny lines about her eyes. She was probably almost thirty-seven and made no attempt to conceal it. Her skin had that faint glow which comes, he ironically surmised, from health, and fresh spring water.

But here, without warning, his physical resources yielded to the malady which, for the past twenty-four hours, had been steadily invading them. His dizziness suddenly increased, and with it came an almost comic inability to breathe. All at once all extraordinary darkness seemed to rush upon him from the corners of the room. He fell forward in his chair; then utterly collapsed.

Everything after that was a nightmare—a confused impression of figures about him, of flurry, alarm and general upheaval. But the pain in his chest and the surrounding mist swamped it all.

Later, he emerged momentarily to find himself in an upstairs bedroom with a stranger stooping over him: a spare, dry, elderly man with pince-nez, a small gray imperial, and a dangling instrument of metal and rubber which Lennard's dulled consciousness perceived to be a stethoscope.

"Yes," he thought, "I'm going to be really ill." And aloud he gasped: "Get me to a hospital."

But the mist swept down again, and Lennard did not hear the doctor's answer. He heard little during the next ten days but the harsh sound of his own breathing, which echoed in the room like a saw rasping through tough timber and gave him the maddening notion that he was exhausting himself upon some infinite woodpile. During that time he lay gripped by fever and racked by a cough that had its part in the conspiracy to forbid him rest. For the most part, he was delirious, but in the fleeting seconds of lucidity he had an ironic anticipation of his own obituary notices.

Yet one afternoon, as by a miracle, he passed the crisis of his illness. And he became aware of himself lying there in the low bed, painfully weak and emaciated, but pervaded by the cynical recognition that he was alive. He remained passive, his eyes on the elderly trained nurse who stood at the foot of his bed.

"That's right," she murmured. "You feel better now, I guess. But don't talk. Doctor Archer'll be in presently."

Half an hour later Doctor Archer appeared. Though the dry cast of his features betokened a nature habitually reticent, he entered with a brisk self-satisfaction.

"Well, well, Mr. Lennard, it's good to see you yourself again." He rubbed his hands together spryly. "Believe me, you've had a pretty close call. Yes, sir, you gave us something to do these last ten days."

Lennard had a cruel impulse to prick the little man's complacency. "Put it in the bill, then," he answered briefly and, turning over, he went to sleep.

It was next morning when he opened his eyes, a sweet spring morning full of light airs and the gay sound of birds, Neither the nurse nor Doctor Archer was in the room, but by the half-open window Mrs.

Day stood arranging a bowl of fresh-cut flowers. She turned when she saw that he was awake and smiled at him in silence.

Her smile, which seemed effected entirely by her eyes—those clear hazel eyes that shone with such artless and engaging candor—both puzzled and tormented him. He had a restless return of all that hostility he had felt at their first meeting, an almost angry wish to break down her amiability.

"Before you say anything, let me make my apologies for depriving you of the excitement of my funeral."

"Why, you can't know how glad we are that you've pulled through——!" She broke off with a doubtful little gesture, still smiling, yet disturbed by the hard look on his face.

He waited a moment. "All this rejoicing bores me beyond words. I didn't plan to be ill here, and I asked you to send me to a hospital. If yon expect me to be grateful, you're quite mistaken. That kind of sentiment revolts me."

She nodded, her troubled gaze on him. "I think I understand."

"Then the sooner we end an unfortunate situation, the better. Perhaps you'll ask your husband to look in on me this morning?"

She replied quietly: "My husband is in Los Angeles. He had to leave three days ago. He was very sorry. He said we must do everything to get you well."

An exclamation broke from Lennard, half petulant, half perverse, "I *am* well. All I want is to get out of here and back to New York."

"Why, of course," she acquiesced, "whenever you wish, since you're so anxious to go."

Once again the absolute placidity with which she met his rudeness stung him beyond understanding. He bit his lip as she left the room, feeling that for all his superiority she had somehow frustrated and defeated him. He had to fall back upon Archer to vent his ill temper. But the doctor, who called about eleven, had not forgotten the previous rebuff. His manner was as acrimonious as his patient's. He declared with asperity that it was suicide for Lennard to dream of moving until he was stronger.

In his heart Lennard admitted this as common sense, yet though he grudgingly resigned himself to obey Archer, the prospect of another week in this house filled him with a singular exasperation.

On the following two days he did his best to distract himself. Then, one morning, Jones came down from New York bringing correspondence, but he was too fatigued to bother about it.

THAT SAME afternoon he requested the nurse to convey his compliments to Mrs. Day and ask her to look in on him if she had nothing better to do. She came at once and, with a change in his manner, which had been abrupt to the point of insolence, he declared:

"I'm so sorry to bother you but I'm feeling frightfully glum. Would it annoy you to talk to me for a bit?"

She colored, as she did so easily. "I should only bore you."

"How could you possibly think that?"

She smiled. "You're so terribly clever and I'm so terribly dull." But she drew forward a chair and sat down by his bedside.

He exerted himself to be pleasant; and the result was naïve.

Hitherto she had confined herself to one courtesy visit in the day, but now, since he showed signs of appreciating her society, she began to spend more and more time with him. She sat with him, talked, read aloud. She unfolded unsuspectingly under his attention. When he told her with his tongue in his cheek how well she read, she blushed like a young girl and answered that she had often read at home to her mother. At this, with deliberate malice, he pressed her to tell him about herself.

Her name, apparently, was Phoebe. And she was originally from Lerton, Michigan, where her father had been a small-town lawyer. Listening gravely, Lennard had a vision of the frame house, the dilapidated buggy; of fudge parties and choir practice; of gawky youths and giggling girls in spotted muslin—exactly the background from which she must have sprung. At seventeen, she had moved with the family to Milwaukee, and there she had met and straightway married Sam Day, insurance agent for the Fire and General.

What a romance! Lennard had to hold the rein tight upon his laughter as she guilelessly related how the tender flame had burned all these years. Her eyes were kind as she spoke of Sam; he was so decent, so genuine and human. He'd got on marvelously, too, for a man comparatively uneducated, He'd been one of the first to foresee the future of the movies; had worked his way to the front of the Vestris Corporation.

He was away from home a great deal, of course—on the Coast, San Francisco and other places; often for three months at a spell. Naturally, that was hard to put up with, but she accepted it now as part of the conditions of her life. She had no inclination toward the life in California; and anyhow, Sam didn't want her mixed up with the Hollywood clique.

Jonstown suited her to perfection. She was very domesticated, disliked smart restaurants and hotels. She liked running her house, She was a member of the Winnemac, Country Club; gave lessons to the Girls' Guild in the winter; worked all the year round in her garden.

Her story touched the apex of the commonplace. As Lennard listened, he saw her as the perfect exemplar of all the humdrum virtues, the good woman of the Victorian storybook, sweet, industrious, faithful and pure, a type he had hitherto believed more finally departed than the dodo.

"Of course, your one sorrow is that you have no children," he suggested. masking his irony with a careful gravity.

Her eyes fell. "Yes," she sighed. "That's our one regret."

It was too perfect, her unsuspecting response. Now the picture was complete. He had a sudden impulse, restrained only with difficulty, to shock her by some ribald gibe; to outrage this modesty which so infuriated him.

By the end of the week he was able to be up, and on the first day he could hobble out of doors she took him round her garden. He had prepared himself for pergolas and crazy paving, a concrete sundial and a birdbath. But the garden was natural and beautiful, watered by the rushing millstream, to whose edges the soft lawns came, full of flowering cherries and graceful birches, and banked by copses of feathery green pine.

"I've tried to keep it quite unspoiled." Her affection for the place was plain, and as they rounded a bend of the stream, reaching a lower level of the ground, a marshy peninsula where a dozen men were busy untrucking soil and rocks, a look of real pride came into her eyes.

"They're reclaiming it," she explained. "All that was swampland. They're making it good, where it was worthless before. It's a little scheme I have. I get these men from the Relief Organization in New York. Every one of them was walking the streets, destitute, before he came here." She paused. "You see, we're trying to reclaim them, too."

At this crowning example of her bourgeois charity he was viciously silent.

They came back to the house and entered the terrace room, where Rose, the maid, anticipating their return, had just brought in tea.

Though the expedition had been short, he felt played out, and his fatigue was visible in his face. From time to time Mrs. Day glanced at him with genuine concern. Something was on her mind. And at last she said impulsively:

"Mr. Lennard, why don't you stop here a little longer?"

He stared at her, speechless.

"You really aren't well yet," she continued persuasively. "You've just said you liked my garden. Why don't you stay for a week or two and help me with it? Get some real exercise in the open, for a change. It would do you all the good in the world. You know, there isn't any doubt that if you return right away to New York, you're going to get ill again. Doctor Archer was saying—" She broke off abruptly, gazing at him between confusion and entreaty.

His thin lips twisted in cynical amusement. "You've been discussing me with our medical friend. He's full of melodramatic foreboding about what he calls my hectic mode of life."

"Oh, please! You mustn't talk that way. You've been so different lately I would like—"

"To reclaim me, too." he interposed, with sardonic reference to her swampland scheme.

There was a pause. He surveyed her as she sat there, so earnest in her intention, her expression so ingenuous and sweet. And all at once his hostility came to a head in a sudden bitter determination. Why hadn't he thought of it before? It was the only way. He replied in an even voice:

"You're far too kind to me. And I dare say you're right. I do need a rest, a change. I need to be taken in hand by someone who might give me a better, a more normal outlook on life."

"You'll stay, then?" she exclaimed.

"Why, yes. I'd love to stay here for a week or two. It's very lovely." His tone was logical. Even diffident. "But really, your husband—wouldn't he—?"

At first her bewilderment was almost comical; then she laughed. "You don't understand. Why, Sam wouldn't dream of objecting. Oh, it's too amusing!"

"Yes," said Lennard gently, "Amusing is perhaps the word."

He stayed. That evening he rang his apartment in New York. There was considerable businesss demanding his attention, but he shelved everything. He asked merely for some things to be sent down, dismissing Jones' suggestion that the valet should come too. Nothing, he reflected with a sardonic smile, must interfere with his regeneration.

This began on the following day. Despite his weakness it was clear that Mrs. Day meant to be as good as her word. With a serious air she led him across the terrace and introduced him to a pair of light clippers and the hedge which marked the boundary of the lawns.

"This wants trimming," she announced. "You'll probably make a mess of it. But never mind; it makes an easy start."

He did not find it so easy, nevertheless, standing in the sun, working the clippers clumsily.

During that week he was more than once on the point of throwing up the whole affair. From the privet hedge he went to shear some borders of box—a trying task involving much painful recognition of his knees and back. On Thursday, Mrs. Day put him on the lawns where, with increasing venom, he pushed a mower to and fro. Only the thought of her ultimate humiliation held him to it. Images rose in his mind and he dwelt upon them with grim satisfaction as he sweated behind the whirring machine.

HIS HANDS grew blistered and his skin tanned, and at night he rolled uneasily in bed in the effort to ease the anguish of his unaccustomed muscles. But by Saturday he was digging, actually digging, in the garden! Just after she came to him and stood watching, a faint smile on her lips.

"You're doing famously," she said at length. "But do be careful of my lily of the valley." He stared at the clump of unflowering green shoots near which he had driven the spade. "They don't do so well here," she added, "but for all that, they're my favorite flower."

"Your favorite?" he repeated, stung by the odd

softness of her tone. "Why?"

She colored under the directness of his question, but made no effort to evade it. "Sam used to send me lily of the valley—when we first met. He still does occasionally, when he's missing me a lot. It's then I know how much Sam and I mean to each other. That it counts so much."

He made no answer, but in a sulky silence accompanied her in to lunch. Her tender, absurd association of the lily of the valley with her husband's love had grossly provoked him. He helped himself to fried chicken, herb stuffing and sweet corn from the platter presented by Rose, then to homegrown potatoes mashed and buttered. His appetite was ravenous. Several times he came back for more.

He sighed at last, and raising his eyes from his plate, found hers bent quizzically upon him.

"Some more stuffing?" she suggested.

At the friendly humor in her tone his ill temper left him. He had to laugh, a perfectly natural laugh which startled him by its spontaneity.

"A great improvement," she went on. "It's good to hear you laugh like that."

He lighted a cigaret and stretched luxuriously. "Do I have to work Saturday afternoon?"

She shook her head, smiling, "It's the hired man's half day. Would you like to come fishing?"

"Fishing?" he echoed, rather blankly.

They went, nevertheless, launching a punt on the lake lying in the nest of woods to the east of the property—a lovely stretch of water leased by the Winnemac Country Club. He understood nothing of angling but he saw plainly that Mrs. Day knew what she was doing.

His mind was in a state of unusual quiescence, his senses soothed by the slow lapping of the water against the gunwale, by the play of light and shadow on the lake, the aromatic scents of pine and birch. How young she looked! She was like a young girl. Her old bleached blouse, open at the neck, showed her sun-browned skin. The line of her hip was firm under the short linen skirt. In such surroundings the simile came easily to mind: she looked clean as the spring-fed lake and as free from artifice.

Though they talked little, the long afternoon passed quickly. She caught all good-sized bass.

"You shall have them for dinner. Then you'll see how good they are." She added: "Doctor Archer is coming."

It annoyed him that the doctor should be there, yet the edge of his exasperation was no longer keen. He dressed carefully that night, feeling an exhilaration in his sun-drenched body. As he knotted his bowtie, his reflection in the glass did not displease him. His eye was clear, his cheek brown; for the first time in years he looked fit.

"Making a man of yourself at last," he mocked his image, adding with cynical derision: "With the help of God and a good woman."

Archer, however, was solemnly of that opinion.

After a quick appraising glance, his manner toward Lennard was less brusque.

The dinner was a success. The French windows of the long, cool room were open to the rushing millstream. Maggie had made a symphony of the bass. And the new moon rose above the old millhouse and looked in upon them.

They were taking coffee in the terrace room when, unexpectedly, an urgent call was phoned through from Doctor Archer's house. Though he gave no sign, a thrill went over Lennard. The old doctor rose grumblingly, promising to return later if he could; then surreptitiously Lennard glanced at Mrs. Day. It was an opportunity at last. Rising, he went over to the grand piano which stood in a raised embrasure at the end of the room.

"Do you play?" he asked.

She shook her head. "No, I'm not nearly good enough. But I love it."

He sat down and, gazing toward her over the ebony surface of the grand piano, he began to play softly. A lovely melody flooded the room.

A sigh broke from her when he finished and she turned to him, entranced. "That was lovely, lovely. I'd no idea you could play like that. Please, what was it?"

"Oh, something of my own. A melody I'm thinking out for my next operetta."

It was clear that his negligent words profoundly impressed her. A touch of awe was in her tone, "How wonderful to have that gift! But you have so many gifts, Mr. Lennard."

"Why Mr. Lennard? Aren't we Gilbert and Phoebe to each other now?"

"Why, yes," she said slowly, "if you wish it—Gilbert."

He did not answer but, still holding her eyes, he began gently, almost caressingly, to play the "Liebestraum." As the liquid notes melted through the quiet room she listened, enchanted, and when he finished an almost painful silence followed. He saw that her eyes were filled with tears.

"How lovely!" she whispered.

"It's the 'Liebestraum,' " he answered. "Liszt wrote it."

Silence again, an electric stillness. She was deeply moved, her face upturned toward him, her expression strangely bewitched. She had the look of a dove unconsciously fascinated by some sinister and unknown force.

For a moment he kept his dark eyes upon her; then slowly he rose. But as he moved toward her, the door opened and Archer walked back into the room.

"A false alarm," he announced. "I don't have to go, after all. And now let's shoot some three-handed bridge."

Lennard's face made an ugly study. Willingly he would have shot the unsuspecting doctor.

Four days elapsed, and Lennard tried hard but unsuccessfully to recreate in Mrs. Day the moment of emotion which had been so rudely shattered. His own intensity amazed him. Everything he had he concentrated to break down her reserves.

"You know," he remarked with apparent idleness—"forgive me for mentioning it—but it does strike me as queer, your hearing so little from your husband."

"Yes?" She smiled at him with the utmost frankness. "Well, I don't think it strange. You see, I understand Sam. As a matter of fact, I haven't heard from him since he left. But that doesn't make the slightest difference. Sam and I mean everything to each other."

"The perfect marriage, eh?" The sneer escaped him.

"Why not?" she answered simply.

"But doesn't it ever strike you that Sam may be—well, shall I say, amusing himself occasionally on the Coast?"

"Possibly," she said calmly. "But does it matter?"

Her devotion to her mediocre husband infuriated him, yet more than ever it hardened his determination. He redoubled his efforts to seduce her.

During the next two days nothing of note took place, but on the evening following, the invitation to the dance arrived. It was no more than the usual monthly dance at the country club but Lennard snatched at the opportunity.

"Would it compromise you if I came I along?"

"What?" Her surprise was obvious. "This dance? Oh, really, you couldn't be bothered with that."

"I could—if you were there."

"But I hardly ever go," she protested.

"Please." He bent forward with only half-concealed eagerness. "I've been pretty good, haven't I, doing everything you've asked? Now I'm asking this little thing of you. I want us to go to this dance. I haven't had any fun since I've been ill. Now I'm really well. I want us to have a celebration. It'll be my evening. I owe you something, surely, for what you've done for me."

"Well..." She temporized, feeling for the first time a little alarmed. But his manner of asking had made it impossible for her to refuse.

From the moment she agreed to go, he began to build up subtly on the dance. He made himself charming, attentive, gay. His manner infected her.

"It's absurd," she remarked. "You keep on romancing about this dance, and I haven't a rag to wear."

Struck by an idea, he replied instantly: "I should love to choose you a dress—something really worthy of you."

She laughed. "Don't tell me you add dress designing to your other accomplishments!"

Yet Lennard had no intention of dismissing the matter as a joke. That same evening he made use of the wire to New York, and on the following afternoon a thin dark woman arrived in a large automobile. Three dresses came with her.

Lennard had hoped to pass things off without disclosing the identity of this unexpected visitor—she was Madame Nina, who dressed most of his productions—but he couldn't. After a moment of complete incredulity, Mrs. Day was hurt and angry.

"How could you dream of taking such a liberty!" she exclaimed.

Lennard protested that he had not meant to offend her. "I tell you I'm sorry," he muttered for the tenth time.

Then she perceived that he seemed genuinely upset. Her mood changed suddenly. "Very well, then," she said in a softer tone. "Perhaps it's stupid to make such a fuss. Since she's here, I'll see her. But If I choose one of those expensive models, I shall pay for it myself."

"Pay!" he echoed. "What does that matter, so long as you look beautiful?"

And at the blank logic of his tone the situation was suddenly reversed. She flushed, then her eyes, searching his face in a kind of wonder, filled with apprehension. Nothing more was said about the dress, even after Nina had gone.

The evening of the dance fell still and warm. Lennard was ready early, and with unusual restlessness sat waiting by the wide windows of the terrace room, from which position he commanded a view of the hall and staircase. Every minute be kept glancing at the brass face of the long case clock. His impatience made the measured beats of the swinging pendulum seem painfully slow.

AT LAST she came downstairs and through the hall. She wore the dress his fancy had created for her—a parchment gray, the skirt full and long, the bodice cut in a low plain sweep from which her neck rose slenderly. Her beauty, now made fully manifest, was greater far than he had expected. He rose and advanced to meet her.

"Why," he murmured, "you take my breath away!'

She flushed. How easily she flushed now when he spoke to her! And then he saw that she was nervous. She was pale, and her hand trembled as she pulled on her glove. The knowledge filled him with confidence, made him gay.

"Let's go now," he said, smiling, "I can't bear to miss a single dance."

They drove to the club. It was not remarkable, but the grounds were strung prettily with colored electric lights. A great many people were there—the dance floor was filled with a hilarious crowd. Ordinarily the scene would have bored Lennard, but tonight he was only half conscious of the bright background; of numbers of people who greeted Mrs. Day affectionately, then shook him by the hand.

And then he was dancing with her, holding her in his arms. She was not a practiced dancer, yet she was extraordinarily light on her feet. The rhythm of the music beat sensuously. He talked to her as they danced, intimately. He used all his charm, and gradually, almost unwillingly, he felt her respond. The slight resistance left her body. She smiled at him timidly.

"Are you enjoying this?" he murmured.

"You know I am."

They danced again and again. He brought her a glass of champagne but she refused it. And then, as they stood at the edge of the open portico, he said:

"I'm so sorry I must go away tomorrow."

Watching her narrowly, he saw the piteous light that flashed into her eyes.

"Tomorrow!" she gasped.

He nodded his head, filled by a sense of bitter triumph. He knew now that the end of his long pursuit was in sight.

"Are you sorry?"

A silence.

"Yes."

The unwilling monosyllable which held such a rich essence of meaning excited him. He reached out and took her hand. And then, as they stood there, the band broke into the hit number from his last year's show, "Spanish Highway." It was a haunting tune. She looked at him with dimmed eyes.

"We must dance this," she whispered.

They swung out on the softly lighted veranda. He felt that it was the moment.

"Of course you know that I love you," he said in a low voice.

At first he thought she had not heard. She did not answer. Then he became aware of the trembling of her body. They continued to dance, instinctively, as though floating in some strange air, but when the music ceased she said stiffly:

"I think I want to go home now."

They drove back in dead silence under a great moon which filled the night with a white and dewy luster. After the loud brightness of the club, the quiet of the house came like a caress.

He entered the terrace room, which was filled by the magic mist of the all-pervading moonshine. She stood in the doorway, outlined against the lighted hall exquisitely steeped in silver and shadow, like a portrait by Whistler. Not looking at him, she said:

"You'll have a drink before you turn in?"

He held his two hands toward her with a practiced gesture. "You heard what I said, didn't you? I love you."

Instinctively she pressed her hand to her side. There was a long pause; then slowly her fluttering eyelids lifted. She took a step into the room.

She whispered brokenly: "And the awful thing is . . . that I love you, too."

The next instant they were together, his lips against hers. How sweet her kiss was; how unbelievably innocent! Under that kiss his bitter triumph died and all his affectation deserted him. His heart contracted with unbelievable emotion. On the low couch she clung to him like a child, white and defenseless, Through tears she repeated, again and again:

"I love you. Darling, I love you. Nothing matters but that—nothing."

He did not move but remained like a man stunned

by some fantastic thunderbolt. With inconceivable poignancy he knew that he loved her; that for the first time in his bored, artificial life, cluttered with innumerable tawdry affairs, he had fallen deeply and genuinely in love. He had begun by desiring her from malice, but now the paradox was inverted and it was love which finally restrained him. He shivered faintly. It was an emotion greater than any he had ever known.

As she lay in his arms, quieter, he could feel her gratitude, her happiness.

"We must go away," she whispered. "We can't wait here, in this house. We'll go away tomorrow. Oh, you love me, don't you, darling?"

"You know I do," he answered.

"Then we'll begin to live." She gave a sob. "Oh, I can't help myself. Don't think I don't know what I'm doing, darling. Nothing matters if we are together."

"Nothing."

"I'm so happy," she whispered. "I never knew such happiness could be. When I think of the future I could cry for joy. Oh, you're so sweet to me, darling. You've changed so much."

HE STROKED her hair gently, mastering the hurt her words gave him. He knew he had not changed. He would never change. In one devastating flash the glory slipped from the romantic vision and he was confronted by bare reality. In that moment he looked into his own soul.

Fundamentally, he was quite worthless. This idealism was momentary. The phase would pass, and he would be himself again—cold, cynical, hopelessly unreliable. Then he would tire of her; yes, he would break her heart, bring her not happiness but eternal sorrow.

"Why are you so quiet, darling?"

"Thinking of all the things we'll do together," he answered tenderly.

It was late when she left him, kissing him lightly before she slipped from his arms and vanished upstairs.

He sat for a long time when she had gone, his thin face lighted by the afterglow of her presence. At last he rose and went to his room.

Next morning he was down early. He entered the breakfast room and, as he had expected, she was there. She smiled as he entered and shyly held up her face. He kissed her.

"Did you sleep well?" she asked, when she had given him coffee.

"Pretty fair." He smiled at her intimately. "Did you?"

She shook her head gaily. "I was too happy, thinking of our going away."

He laughed. "I've been all worked up about it, too. Had to take a run-around before breakfast to cool off."

"Darling!"

Five minutes later Rose, the maid, entered. She carried a long parcel under her arm. "It just came by special messenger, ma'am," she announced. "From New York, he said."

When Rose had gone, Mrs. Day stripped the wrappings from the box and lifted the lid. Then a cry of distress broke from her lips.

"Sam!" she gasped. The box was filled to the brim with lovely lily of the valley.

Her gaze remained fixed upon the exquisitely pure flowers for what seemed an eternity of time; then she faced Lennard. Her eyes were filled with tears.

"From Sam," she repeated in a tormented voice. "To think he should send them today! If it had been anything else!" And then, desperately, as she broke into scalding tears: "Leave me, darling—just for a little. I'll be all right, but I want to think—about Sam . . ."

An hour later Lennard left for New York, alone. The same day he canceled all his American arrangements and booked his solitary passage on a boat which sailed for Southampton that night. But before he left he permitted himself a sentimental pilgrimage. He went in person to the florist's on Park Avenue to pay for the lily of the valley.

MASCOT FOR UNCLE

WHEN UNCLE and I first saw Kitch, he was sitting on the slimy stone steps passing the time philosophically by seeing how far he could spit. He was waiting for us. It was very dark in the tenement, and outside a dirty fog had been hanging over Edinburgh all day. But from what I could make out Kitch was just about the worst case I had ever seen. The rickets in that district—all over those condemned slum areas, in fact—was terrible. Starvation and lack of sunlight—that was the trouble. You had only to look at Kitch to see it. He sat there with his twisted legs curled under him and his crooked little back sagging forward as though it were broken. He was so small his head seemed three sizes too big for him and too heavy to hold up. He held it up with one hand, bracing his elbow, that was sharp as a gimlet, against his knee. His eyes were enormous in his pinched face. His skin was the color of wax. He was almost transparent. He didn't seem to wear any clothes—just bits and pieces mostly held together with string. He looked like a tired old man. He was six.

Sitting there, he took us all in with his big grave eyes, rather wearily knowing us, knowing about the black bag Uncle was lugging along.

"Is it Aggie Dodds yous is wantin'?"

Staring at Kitch, Uncle nodded.

"Haulf a mo', then, an' I'll show yous."

Kitch got up. He did this like all rickety kids, holding onto his legs and struggling as though he were climbing up himself. It was quite a job. But at last it was done. Out of breath already, he led the way upstairs. It was a miracle to me how he dragged himself along at all.

The stair was no worse than ordinary. Half the banisters were gone, torn off for firewood or fights. There were no windows, light, or air. These back-to-back tenements are always like that. The gas brackets were plugged, a cracked pipe had drenched one landing.

On the top landing Kitch turned back right into his house. From the way Kitch behaved you could see it was his house. It was a single room. Doing our cases, Uncle and I had seen a hundred rooms like that. We were not astonished. This was just the average. The woman who was going to have the baby lay on a dirty mattress stretched upon the bare boards. Beside her, on an upended egg box, drinking red biddy, was a fat woman in a shawl, with her black hair hanging all bedraggled down her back. In the near corner four kids were playing with the lid of an old tin can. There was no furniture, only a kettle, some sacking, and a bashed-in wash-basin.

Kitch went over to the woman on the bed. She was his mother.

"Hey, Aggie," he said, jerking his head toward us. "They're here!"

The fat neighbor on the egg box slued round. "Holy God, Kitch, ye've brung the medicals. Holy God, but yer a cliver one!"

Kitch took no notice whatever, nor, for that matter, did we. She was far gone, the fat one, drunk as a lady—red biddy, a mixture of methylated spirits and port, is knockout stuff. I took off my jacket and rolled up my sleeves. I took the bag from Uncle and began getting out the instruments. Uncle still seemed to be staring at Kitch. I had never seen him like that before. He seemed absolutely taken with Kitch and the way Kitch was managing things. He watched Kitch bring over the kettle which stood on the spark of fire, collect the four younger kids and put them out to play on the landing, then tug commandingly at the fat woman's shawl.

"Out ye come, Lizzie Broun. Ye're no' wanted here."

"Oh, Jasus, lemme be, Kitch."

Unexpectedly Uncle came out of his trance to go to Kitch's assistance. "Yes, out you go, missus."

"Oh, Jasus," said the woman. "Them students!"

But she went.

And Kitch, with a last look round and a grave little nod, went after her. Then Uncle and I got on with the job. But for some reason Uncle was less on with the job than usual. He hardly even looked at what he was doing. And usually Uncle was so conscientious he made you want to kick him.

Uncle was a queer devil. His real name was Spiers—David Murdoch Spiers. He was a chronic. He was the prize chronic. For seventeen years he had been at the University trying to take his medical degree. You had to know about this to believe it. Twelve times now he had come up for his final, and every time they had flunked him. It was Pollock, the surgery professor, who usually ditched him. Uncle said that Pollock was down on him, but nobody believed that for a minute. Uncle was so stupid. He was absolutely dense. He had less brain than a sheep. But he would not give up. It was painful. He plodded on, working himself dizzy, trying, trying, trying to get through. He wanted to be a doctor. He must get his degree. He must. You see, Uncle had religion, and the sole object of his life was to go to China as a medical missionary.

He was a lumpy, awkward, moon-faced man with a stoop. He walked inclined slightly forward, as if he was always in a hurry. His eyes behind his round steel-rimmed glasses were glued on the ground. He gave you the idea of being plunged in thought, but what he thought about only God knew. He had big feet. He seemed to be falling over himself. His lips moved, repeating the things he had learned and would not remember. Under his arm he carried a pile of books. Whenever he sat down, he opened one of the books. His expression was both worried and earnest. And nervous, too. A loud noise made him jump out of his skin. He was nearly forty years of age. He was the butt of the whole Medical School. They called him Uncle. He was comic. He was comic history.

Uncle had no friends, but I fell in with him, slightly to my surprise, because we were both so hard up. Everyone thought Uncle was stingy. He had one rusty black suit of clothes that he wore in all weathers. He did not drink or smoke or play billiards or belong to the Students' Union. He was a complete outsider. But one day in the winter term I found out about Uncle. We were dissecting. It was late, and all the others had gone. The anatomy room was very chilly. I felt like packing up myself, and without thinking I asked Uncle to drop over with me for a coffee. He looked up from his work, and to my amazement his eyes slowly filled with tears.

"That's the first decent thing that's been said to me for weeks."

I felt sick somehow. "Oh, shut up, man, and come on out for your coffee."

He shook his head solemnly. "I'd like to. But I can't. It's against my principles. I've made it a rule never to accept anything I can't pay back."

I stared at him in disgust. He must have read my

face, for with that same heavy priggishness he laid down his scalpel, put his hands in his trousers pockets, and pulled out the lining. Both pockets were quite empty. He hadn't a bean on him. Still watching my face, he let out his harsh laugh. It was like a bray.

"That's how I am all the term."

He paid for his digs beforehand; at least, his cousin, a crofter in Ullapool up in the West Highlands, squared this for him. His fees were settled from the same source. And from the croft he took a bag of meal and a sack of potatoes. That did him till he went back.

After this it somehow became less funny seeing Uncle ragged. Frew, Dallas, and Stobo were always at him. They were the bloods of my year, all pretty smart at their work besides being good at games and ready to fling their cash around. Frew's old man, who had a handle to his name, was a big pot on the City Council and rolling in money through graft and council contracts. And young Frew especially ragged Uncle. One day he pinned a notice on Uncle's back, "I'm on my way to China," and Uncle walked about all day with that notice on his back, everybody laughing—even Prof Pollock in the surgery clinic laughing at the poor dumbbell. And Uncle never knew about it until he pulled off his coat to go to bed. Next day I hoped he would hit Frew a sock on the jaw. But Uncle never even mentioned it.

It was a pity. For Uncle had guts of a kind. I saw this plainly enough when I went to dig with him. That was in my final year, when the money left for my education by my father had nearly run out and I was pretty hard up against it. I really did not like Uncle much, and I'm afraid he did not care a lot about me. But this time it was a plain case of living as cheaply as possible. And when it came to that kind of economics, I felt Uncle could show me the way. And he certainly did. I went fifty-fifty with Uncle on another bag of oatmeal, and since then have never been able to look a plate of porridge in the face. I also took out my confinement cases with him. And it was on the case at Seventeen Clyde Place that we met Kitch.

I admit I forgot all about Kitch. On the day after, Uncle said,

"I'll do Seventeen Clyde Place if you like."

But I didn't think anything of that; we had so many visits to those lying-in cases we usually split them. Anyhow, Uncle appropriated Seventeen Clyde, and I didn't realize there was a reason until a week later. It was evening, and we were sitting at the table in our digs boning hard. At least I was boning when I heard Uncle say,

"The thing is, he hasn't had a chance."

I looked up. The dreamy expression on his face was so idiotic I just stared at him.

"Who hasn't had a chance?"

Uncle blinked at me. He had been talking his thoughts out loud. He reddened. "It's Kitch. Don't you remember him?"

Once it was out, you could see he wanted to talk

about the kid. He went on. I had never heard him so lay-me-down-and-die before.

"He's made a powerful impression on me, that child. He's extraordinary. He's just a little bundle of deformed bones. You saw it yourself. He can hardly walk. He's half-starved. He's never seen a green field or had a breath of fresh air in all his life. He's never known anything but that sink of squalor and corruption. And yet he never so much as lets a whimper out of him. It's—oh, man, it's an inspiration."

Uncle was certainly wound up. But when he took the pulpit this way, he always left me cold.

"Go easy, Uncle. The kid's only one of ten thousand. You ought to know that's how they sprout in our garden city."

He wouldn't have it. "No!" He started to stammer the way he did when he got excited. "He's different! He's a wonder. Six years old, and he faces the world like a man. You ought to see the way he's been looking after his mother and his little brothers and sisters. He makes the tea and spreads the bread. He's sharp as a needle. He knows everybody in the street. He goes all the errands. He even goes to the pub for beer. He runs lines to the bookie. Just think of it! Six years old. And the language he's picked up. Oh, it's infernal, man! He ought to have a better chance. And let me tell you this—I'm the one who'll give him that chance. When I get through, I'll send him to the country. I'll get him strong again. I'll straighten out his poor little limbs. I'll do it! The minute I'm qualified."

I saw it was useless arguing. Some crazy notion had got under Uncle's hat. He had about as much chance of qualifying as Hitch had of ever getting well. Absolute zero. I knew the statistics on these slum kids. Not one in ten got through. It was written all over them. And if ever a face bore the hallmark of Kingdom Come, it was Kitch's bony little mug. But what was the good of talking? I got on with my studying. And so, in fact, did Uncle.

THREE WEEKS later I came out the door of the digs and ran right into Kitch. This time he was sitting on the curb with his curled-up feet resting in the gutter. He always took the chance to sit down when he could, it was so hard for him to stand up. And in any case he must have walked quite a bit to reach our section of the city.

"Hello, Kitch! What in thunder are you doing here?"

He turned his big eyes on me. He was friendly. Maybe because it was a fine day he looked better. He still had his bare feet, but in place of his tied-together rags he had on a little patched pair of pants and a darned woolen jersey.

He jerked his hand toward the house.

"He's takin' me out in the Kelvingrove Park."

"Who?"

"Spiers. Him you call Uncle."

The information set me back a mile, but I covered

it up the best I could. "Anyhow, you're certainly dressed up, Kitch."

"I'm no' so bad." He smoothed the ridiculous pants reflectively. "He gi'en us boots as weel, but Aggie got haud o' them."

"How d'you mean, Kitch?"

"Oh, she's out on a bat again. And this mornin' she up and pawned them."

There was a pause. Somehow his matter-of-course manner made me feel bad. I changed the subject quickly.

"By the way, how do they come to call you Kitch?"

"I'm named after Lord Kitchener. Him what bate the Boers. Aggie says the old man was out on a week's bat when she had me. She didna want it. But he would call me Kitchener Colenso Dodds. I'm no' carin'. Kitch does me fine."

"Where's your old man now, Kitch?"

"Him! Och, he's in the nick. Barlinnie Prison. He got six months for knockin' hell out o' Copper McLeod."

"So Uncle's looking after you now?"

"He is that. He's a gent. Yesterday he gi'en us a penny for no' callin' my wee sister names."

"He's reforming you, eh, Kitch?"

"He's took chairge o' me. When he gets to be a doctor, him and me's goin' to do things like."

I left it at that, for I had to be at Outpatients' before three. But the idea of Uncle playing dry nurse to

Kitch stuck in my head in a bothering kind of way. It was clear he had taken a violent fancy to the kid. And that in itself was queer. Uncle, to my knowledge, had never in all his life thought of anyone but Uncle. And, of course, what he would do to the heathen when he finally reached China.

But I was too busy to puzzle it out. The final was in June, and as the weeks dropped away I was working as I never had worked before. And then, one day in May, as I passed the Union, I saw a crowd on the steps. They were getting a laugh out of something, and it seemed a pretty big laugh. Frew, who was in the middle of them, called me over.

"Here, old man! You ought to be in on this!"

I stopped and went across, rather cautious. Actually Frew wasn't a bad sort. He had been at my prep school and played football with me. I was captain of the side then, and Frew had been glad to know me. He was still glad to know me. But Frew's gold cigarette case and silk shirts and overtailored suits got in the way between us.

"What's up?"

Frew took me by the arm, grinning all over his face. "You haven't heard?"

Stobo, who was in the crowd, couldn't hold it back. He guffawed. "It's your stable companion. It's the funniest thing in years."

Frew cut in. "Shut up, Stobo. Let me tell it." With a struggle he took the grin off his face. He pretended he was serious. He was more than serious. "Old chap, we have reason to suspect that Uncle has become a father!"

A regular roar went up. With the grin back on his face, Frew passed me the photograph. It was a snapshot taken in the Park. It was comic. There was Uncle, clumsy as an elephant, pushing a rickety little gocart in which lay Kitch. The tableau was a scream. And underneath someone had written "Father and child both doing well!"

Everyone was talking, telling me about it, how Dallas had spotted the pair in Kelvingrove and stalked them with his camera. Clever devil, Dallas! They waited for me to laugh. Now they were all watching my face. They seemed to think it funny I did not laugh. I was doing them out of something by not laughing. But I couldn't laugh, not for the life of me. I couldn't even smile. I felt empty inside. I said slowly,

"You've got this wrong."

"Ah, what the hell!" Frew protested. "Have you gone holy Willie, too? It's the joke of the century. I'm posting this up on the notice board toot sweet."

HE HAD just said it when somebody who had been listening at the edge of the crowd shouldered forward.

"Give me that!"

I swung round. It was Uncle. Not that you would have recognized him. He was veal-white. His eyes were staring at the photograph. His lips were twitching so much he could hardly speak.

Frew winked at the rest of them. Cool as you like, he said, "You run away and play, Uncle—I mean Father."

I felt that empty pity for Uncle again. But only for a minute. Something happened. Uncle suddenly got bigger. He snatched the photo out of Frew's hand. He bawled, in his excited stammer:

"You're a dirty hound, Frew. It's all lies. And if you don't shut up, I'll smash you!"

The change in Frew's face would have made a cat laugh. His mouth fell open. He had nothing to say. And neither had the others. They just looked at Uncle as he stuffed the photo in his pocket and barged away.

Uncle never talked about this to me. And I didn't mention it, either. But it sent him up in my estimation a lot. We were round the last bend now and into the straight for the final. June came in unusually hot. But even without the heat it was killing work. I wouldn't wish that examination even on my worst enemy. You have medicine, surgery, and midwifery all in a heap, with written papers, practicals, and orals, by way of top dressing. You have all the clinicals, the operative stuff, and microscopic work as well. And if you flunk in one of them, you flunk in the lot. If there's anything nearer to a nightmare, I don't know about it.

That's how it took me, at any rate. But for some reason or another Uncle seemed to take it very calmly. He slogged at it, of course; late into the nights. And he had all the chronic dodges—cold towels round the head, little notebooks of mnemonics, tables of incubation periods, indexes of symptoms, even stupid little rhymes written round the principal fevers so he could memorize them better. But for all that he was calm. He was sort of supernatural.

IT GOT on my nerves at last, for by this time I was feeling none too gay about my own prospects. And late one night as we sat in our stuffy twelve-by-ten with the window wide open, letting in the used-up city air, I shot off at him:

"Hey, you fat idiot! What do you think you are? Buddha?"

He was sitting with a towel round his head and such an all's-right-with-the-world look on his moon face I could have kicked him. He came out of his trance to say,

"Eh?"

"You're too happy, Uncle. Doesn't this exam mean anything to you?"

He nearly smiled. Or maybe he was just pitying me. "You don't know how much it means." He stopped, then decided to tell me. "As a matter of fact, it means everything. My cousin—" He stopped again. "My cousin has written to me. He cannot pay for me any more. This is my last chance."

I stared at Uncle. I saw what he meant. The back of the Ullapool crofter was finally broken. This time, if Uncle didn't connect with his ticket, he was home on the farm for good. No China, no help the lepers, no fast conversions of the heathen. I still stared at him. Why was he so gay?

He answered it himself. I had never heard him so solemn or presanctified.

"Don't worry. I know I'm going to get through."

I laughed. I simply couldn't help it. "Had a vision, I suppose? Or did somebody read your teacup?"

"Don't sneer, my friend. Even if you want to, please don't sneer. There are things in heaven and earth beyond our understanding."

Good God, I thought, has the man gone balmy? Surely he hadn't gone that way. I lit a cigarette to hide what I was feeling. He was still talking.

"I know I'm getting through this time because I've been told."

"Who told you?"

"Kitch."

"Kitch!"

He nodded, solemn as a judge. "In his own way. It's hard to explain. When I met that child, something happened to me. I'm different. I've got new strength. Call it conviction if you like. But it's more like revelation. I believe God works out things His way. He meant Kitch and me to help each other. That's why we met. Kitch knows it. He says he's my mascot. He knows I can't help him till I get through. That's why I will get through!" He got quite glassy about the eyes, and his voice dropped to a whisper. " 'And a little child shall lead them.' Dear God Almighty, how true that is!"

That stump sermon of Uncle's and the gush that went with it worried me awfully. My own nerves were ragged with the heat and overwork and worry. I was certain Uncle had run into a spot of brain fatigue. But what could I do? I couldn't argue or excite him. I did what I thought best. And that was nothing.

The week went, and Monday arrived. The examination was due to begin on Wednesday. I worked like a dog all Monday, but when it came to Tuesday, I couldn't do another stroke. I was all in. The heat was stifling. I felt as if I had the flu. It was an epidemic that had hit the city and hit it downright hard. In fact, it was a pandemic. It had come right across from Russia, by way of the Balkans, Italy, and Spain. And since Spain was, so to speak, the last port of call, they named it the Spanish flu. It was like the plague. It turned you a funny shade of green, and the next day you were dead. The hospitals were jammed with it.

All this shows how morbid I was feeling. I took my temperature. It was normal. I decided I hadn't got the flu. At the same time I decided I must have twenty-four hours off or go crazy. I still had a little money left. I went in to Uncle.

"We're going into the country today. You know. Trees and cows and grass and dandelions. We need it."

He looked at me stolidly. He surprised me by agreeing. "It would freshen us up for tomorrow. Only . . ."

"Only what?"

"Only I'd like to take Kitch."

I groaned. Then I thought, "What's the difference?" It would be a mad expedition in any case.

WE LEFT the digs and collected Kitch. That was easy. Kitch had never belonged to anyone, and now he belonged to Uncle. It was pathetic to see how these two liked each other. Kitch with his little paw in Uncle's fist and reaching not much above his knee and ricketing along beside him—it was a sight. I didn't exist, except to pay the fares. We went by tram—all the way from smoky Argyll Street down to the very shores of Loch Lomond itself.

Down there it was heavenly. There was a blue sky and a cool breeze, and the sweet sound of the water made you feel good. We lay on the clean white shingle. The loch came lopping to our feet in little waves. I forgot about the *bacillus coli* and the *anastomoses* of the median basilic vein. I felt at peace.

Kitch was quiet now. All the road down he had talked his little head off. He never knew the colors of things could be so bright. A brown horse frisking by a white gate, the river steamboats with their vermilion funnels—oh, it was great. "Look! Look!" he kept saying. Nothing like this had ever happened to him before. No, not ever.

I fell asleep in the sun. When I woke, it was nearly three o'clock. I saw that Uncle and Kitch had been paddling in the loch. Uncle in his shirt-sleeves, with his trousers rolled up above his knees, looked like something out a comic strip. He was rubbing Kitch's bare legs with his hands, massaging them. He was telling Kitch how they would be straight one day, and strong. And Kitch was looking up at Uncle with his big trusting eyes. I hate sentiment; it gives me a pain in the neck. But something in the sight of these two caught me hard. As usual I passed it off by trying to be funny. I turned on my side.

"What d'you see in him, Kitch?"

He eyed me suspiciously. Anything that sounded against Uncle always made him sit up. "A lot more nor I see in you."

I had to laugh. "I believe you've adopted him, Kitch. He says you're getting him through the exam."

"So I am."

"Can you do anything for me?"

"Am no' tryin'."

I got up. I decided that after that we'd better go and feed. We had a high tea at the Balloch Hotel: ham and eggs and oatcakes and jelly and ginger snaps and scones. Kitch's face when he saw that grub was a treat. He couldn't eat much. But what he did eat certainly went well. Afterward we loafed around the pier looking at the swans and the houseboats and the men fishing. The stars were beginning to come out when we caught the tram home.

NEXT MORNING the final began. There is no use describing it. Once that kind of examination starts, you don't know what is happening. You sit in a big hall, with your feet like ice, writing like mad until a bell rings. You don't know what you have written. You go out and smoke a cigarette, shivering, then you come back and do it all over again. I am always a pessimist during any exam. And right away in this one I had a vague idea that I was sunk. But Uncle was on top of the world. He told me he was doing great papers. I couldn't quite see it. Once or twice, when we went over the answers, I saw he was yards out in places. In fact, I figured he was giving just about his usual dumb performance. Maybe worse.

By the end of the week we got through with the written word, and the practicals and orals began. These work out a little differently. Instead of a big hall, you enter a small room where some old men with gray beards sit behind a table waiting for you. "Well now, Mr. So-and-So," says one of them, looking at you, very sly, "will you kindly tell us about the *echinococcus?*" If you do tell him, he stops you quick, and another bird weighs in with something else. They don't want to know what you know. Only what you don't know. And sometimes if you have all the answers, they flunk you out of spite.

I went from bad to worse. Uncle went about humming. He told me he was doing it up right. And then Tuesday came. Tuesday was the day we were all afraid of, for on Tuesday Pollock took the surgery orals. I was on at half-past ten, and you may be sure I was there to the tick, for if Pollock hated one thing next to stupidity, it was unpunctuality. The old man and

and his pals grilled me for twenty minutes, then let me go. As I came out, I heard Uncle's name called. Then I heard it again. I looked round the waiting room in a kind of daze. I saw that Uncle wasn't there. For the third time the janitor called Uncle's name, and waited a full minute. Then he stroked with a pencil on his list and called a different name altogether.

All this sounds unimportant. But it wasn't. Not for Uncle. He had missed his surgery oral. Unless something could be done about it, he was flunked. It all came over me with a rush. "Good God," I thought, "what's happened to the man?"

I shot out of the room and made a dash for our digs. They were quite near, in Hill Street. But Uncle wasn't there. Not a sign of him. I got hold of our landlady. She was a sour old dame. I always hated her. But I never hated her worse than at this moment. She bared her false teeth at me. "Mesterr Spiers left the hoose at nine o' the clock. And 'twas ane o' his braw friends frae Clyde Place what fetched him."

Clyde Place, as quick as the tram could take me. Up the broken stairs into the one room. Yes. Uncle was there. He was sitting with his back to the light, bent over the corner.

"Uncle! For heaven's sake, what's got you? You've missed Pollock!"

He slued round. His face seemed made of putty. Dead white. "Don't make so much noise."

"But look here—"

"Be quiet. Can't you see he's sick?"

I came forward. I saw that Kitch lay on the mattress. And I saw right enough that Kitch was sick. The look on his face was enough, the greenish tinge. I had seen it all over the wards that last fortnight. Kitch had the Spanish flu

I turned to Kitch's mother, who stood there with the baby in her shawl and the other kids around her.

"Can't you get him into hospital?"

She cringed. "We tried, doctor, sir. But they're a' full up. The whole place is down wi' it."

I didn't know what to say. I looked at Kitch again. He wasn't really conscious. His breath kept coming in little jerks. He looked all crunched up. He looked like a street sparrow that has got itself run over. His big eyes were fixed on Uncle, never moving. They seemed to be clutching onto Uncle. I saw that his passage was booked. Absolutely booked and paid for. I waited a minute.

"Uncle, don't miss your clinical this afternoon. You can explain then. Maybe you can square it with Pollock."

"Shut your mouth and fetch me some quinine."

I went and fetched it. Then I went on to my clinical surgery. For some reason I was furious. I cursed. I told myself it didn't matter an old boot to me—Kitch or Uncle or anything. But still I cursed. Kitch was going to God, and Uncle was going back on the farm. They were looking out wings for Kitch up aloft, moldy little ones to match up with his crooked little legs. And up in Ullapool they were looking out an extra fork for Uncle to get busy with on the farm.

I DIDN'T see Uncle the rest of that day or that night or the next day either. He must have stayed with Kitch all the time. I showed up for my clinical medicine oral. That was the lot. Yes, that was the last spasm of the exam. We were all finished for better or worse. It was four o'clock. I had a cup of coffee in the Union. I smoked my last cigarette. Then I walked down to Clyde Place.

Uncle was sitting in the exact same spot. You would have thought he hadn't moved except that he was in his shirt-sleeves, and round about him the floor was littered with stuff. Medicine bottles, a basin and towels, cotton wool and brandy. It was always dark in that room, and now it was darker. Uncle sat very still. He seemed sunk into himself. He had a two days' growth of beard on his white moon face. His eyes were all rimmed with red. In his big fist he held Kitch's hand. Then I saw it wasn't really Kitch's hand—just a cold little dead thing. And the real Kitch was stepping out in his secondhand wings elsewhere.

I had a terrible job getting Uncle away. He didn't make any fuss. He didn't have a thing to say. But he was stunned. He was out on his feet. Eventually I dragged him to our digs and persuaded him to get to bed. He lay down with his clothes on, never saying a word, still staring far ahead. I don't think he slept.

Next day it wasn't much better. He got up and shaved and dressed himself. He stayed in his room a long time. I think he was praying. In fact, I know he was praying. But when he came out, he never said a word about Kitch. He talked about other things. It was pitiful. Two days passed like this, then Kitch was buried. It came out that Uncle had written to his cousin, a sort of last appeal. Anyhow he paid for the funeral. It was not a particularly classy funeral. There was just the one cab—for Uncle, Kitch's mother, and me. Somehow I was there. I wanted to be there. The coffin was plain deal. I never realized how small Kitch was till I saw the size of that coffin. In the cab Uncle let it rest on his knees. At the cemetery it was raining hard. Uncle took off his hat and said a prayer. It was a good prayer. I have to own up to it—I was pretty upset. I kept thinking of that day by the lake. Kitch had loved that day so much. The rain got in my eyes. They shoveled in the wet clay. And that was the end of Kitchener Colenso Dodds.

AFTERWARD I walked up to the Union. I felt low. I felt horribly low. I had a coffee to buck myself up. But it tasted bitter in my mouth. At the next table Frew and Dallas and Stobo and a crowd of fellows were celebrating the end of the exam. Frew leaned across to me.

"Come and join us."

"No, thanks."

He laughed. "Not sorrowing for Uncle, are you?"

I looked at him. "What do you mean?"

He laughed again. "You know he shied at the

orals, don't you? He's jugged."

Something got hold of me. Suddenly I hated Frew. He was so smug and well dressed and sure of himself. He had passed the examination before he took it. Perhaps he was clever. But the pull was there on top of that. He was young Frew. He was Sir James' son. His old man knew all the Senate, was hail-fellow-well-met at the University Club. Pollock in particular was his bosom pal. And there was Uncle, poor mug, with not a soul to speak for him.

I jumped up. I probably lost my head. I let go at them. I told them why Uncle had missed his orals. I gave them the whole issue.

Not one of them spoke when I got through. I had hit them. As for Frew, his face was a study. He had brown eyes, rather soft brown eyes. And now they were beaten down and hurt.

"Are you serious?" he asked after a long while.

"Yes, damn you all, I'm serious." And I walked away.

As I went I could feel those eyes of Frew's on me. They were sorry and very thoughtful.

At the digs Uncle was beginning to get his things together. He was going at the end of the week. I could see he was taking it hard. Now that Kitch was finally away, he was getting a true slant on his position. He was done. He was finished. Every minute that passed brought it more and more before him. And I think the worst was that he felt he had made such a horrible fool of himself. All that soft talk.

About mascots, and getting through, and a little child shall lead them.

But there was nothing I could do about it. I was worried enough myself, waiting to know if I was through that blamed exam. One thing I will say in the Senate's favor, they don't keep you waiting for the results. I would know on Saturday.

Saturday came. I hadn't slept all night, so I had no bother about waking in time. At nine o'clock I walked up the hill to the University. As I got there I could see by the crowd round the notice board that the results were already up. My heart was bumping awfully hard. I shoved my way up to the board.

My heart gave an extra bump. I was through all right. They had even given me honors. My eye traveled down the list. Frew had honors, too, but only second class. Dallas had a pass. And Kinloch. And then I nearly had a fit. No, I nearly passed out altogether. Uncle's name was on the list. David Murdoch Spiers. Uncle's name was there. There was no mistake. His name absolutely was on the list.

I felt somebody looking at me. Across the crowd I saw Frew looking at me, grinning and nodding. The noise was terrible. He shouted something—I couldn't hear what. But I understood all right. I understood what Frew, and Frew's old man, had done. "Dear God," I thought, "people aren't so bad after all!"

I turned and tore back to the room. Uncle was there, reading a letter. I never saw such a look on anybody's face. It was a shining look. He knew. He didn't didn't say a word, and neither did I. He just handed me the letter. I read the letter. It was a fine letter. It had the crest of the Senate on the top and the signature of Pollock at the bottom. And it said that owing to the general excellency of Uncle's papers and a special instance of exemplary conduct on Uncle's part which had been brought to the notice of the Senate, his absence at sundry orals was overlooked. He was through.

Uncle was through. I could have jumped to the ceiling. "God help the heathen Chinee now!" I thought. I could have shouted. Oh, I was terribly pleased. I turned to shake hands. But Uncle didn't see my hand. He was sitting at the table. Before him was the go-cart photograph of Kitch. Uncle was staring at that photograph. But I'm sure he didn't see it. He was blubbering so hard.

THE PORTRAIT

IT WAS quite by chance that the Earnshaws met Félix Liseta in Naples. All June they had been gypsying through Italy, winding along the foothills of the Apennines by way of Tivoli and Capua in an old hired car stacked untidily with luggage and Earnshaw's painting gear.

It was all from choice, of course, and not necessity. Rankin Earnshaw, though not yet at the height of his fame, had already achieved an international reputation as a dry-point etcher among discerning collectors. Katrine, his wife, originally Katrine Tessier of New York, had inherited all the money she wanted.

They had been married for four or five years. At the beginning people had laughed and said how impossible it was for such a marriage to last. Katrine was so lovely, temperamental and gay; Rankin so stolid, prosaic and plain. Earnshaw really was an ugly man, bulky and thickset in his figure, with powerful, clumsy hands and a large head. He looked the blunt Yorkshireman he was, his features rugged, skin slightly pitted from acne, hair an untidy mane.

He had met Katrine on his first visit to New York. Van Heger, the sculptor, taken by the new etcher's unassuming manner and attracted, no doubt, by the possibilities of the subject, had made a bronze of Earnshaw's head, which stood, in the usual way, in Arnhem's window on Park Avenue. There Katrine saw it, and it made a deep impression on her.

Katrine bought the bronze and had it sent to her apartment. Its strength fascinated her—the firm molding of the jaw, the wholesome sweep of brow, the kindliness of the deep-set eyes. She stood before it with a childlike reverence. She stroked it secretly with a possessive touch. She could not rest until she met Earnshaw. Six weeks later, she married him.

Now, as they entered the lounge of the Splendide in Naples, she pressed his arm contentedly. "This is nice, Rankin. I'm tired of playing raggle-taggle under the moon. I'd like a drink with ice in it and a bath with bath salts. Expensive bath salts, my dear! I want a small portion of sophistication for a change."

"You'll find tutti-frutti ice cream, postcards of Vesuvius in eruption, and smells in Naples," Earnshaw answered in his dry style. "But no sophistication." He had hardly spoken, however, when he heard his name called, and swinging round, he saw a small, oldish man, with a yellow skin and a highly military white mustache, seated at a table with three others. Earnshaw smiled: "I'm wrong, Katrine. Here's old Brand. And as usual he's in the middle of a party."

They went over, feeling that absurd gratification with which one greets an acquaintance abroad who is merely a bore at home. Colonel Brand was a friend of some years' standing, a New Yorker who spent much of his time between the Lido and the Riviera, a dried-up, pretentious, likable cosmopolite, who dabbled in the finance of art and had a marvelous collection of Renoirs in his brownstone house on Madison Avenue. No one ever knew in what manner or for what reason he had acquired military rank; nevertheless, the appellation stuck and no smart gathering of Americans abroad seemed complete without the colonel as its dapper nucleus.

However, on this occasion it was not his party. He made this clear as he introduced his companions—the Marchesa Ginori, Charley Masters and his host, Félix Liseta.

At the mention of Liseta's name, the Earnshaws gaped slightly and forgivably. Turning, Katrine let her wide eyes rest in startled wonderment upon the smooth-skinned man who had risen with Brand and Masters and now stood returning her gaze with sleek, half-smiling admiration.

"Not *the* Félix Liseta!" she ejaculated with genuine awe.

A tiny shrug of affected nonchalance admitted his spectacular identity. "Why, yes, Madame, I cannot deny it."

He had an exaggerated Continental accent, rolling his *r*'s romantically, and he was wonderfully handsome in a Latin way.

"Oh, Rankin!" groaned Katrine, flopping into a chair. "Why didn't you let me powder my nose properly?"

EVERYONE laughed except Liseta, who bent forward with an operatic air. "I assure Madame she has no cause for regret. Madame's nose could not be more adorable."

More drinks were brought, and the talk turned upon the recent peregrinations of the Earnshaws. Rankin never had much to say, but Katrine, sparkling under Liseta's flattering interest, gave the gayest account of their rambles and of how, tired of ravioli and spaghetti, they hankered for the fleshpots of civilization.

"Then you cannot do better than join us!" cried Liseta. Showing his teeth in a flashing smile, he turned to Earnshaw. "Since we have met so fortunately, I regard you as my guests. You and your most charming wife must come to Capri. Any friend of Colonel Brand's is welcome. We are crossing at five. There! It is agreed."

Earnshaw glanced at Katrine quizzically. Liseta was at that moment such a raging international celebrity and the invitation was so unexpected and flattering that instinctively he demurred.

"It's very kind of you, Mr. Liseta . . ."

"Ah, come. Rankin," urged Brand. "Don't turn down a good time."

"Yes, we'd love to come," breathed Katrine quickly.

It was settled then, with that spontaneity which makes life exciting. And as the time was already close upon five, Earnshaw made a few hurried arrangements about luggage. Then they all left the hotel and walked down the short Via Santa Lucia toward the waterfront. They reached the jetty, where Liseta's yacht, *La Conchita,* awaited them, to find the bay stretching out with exquisite coolness, edged by the blue cliffs of Castellammare, and to see, far off in the hazy distance, shimmering like an opal, the lovely shape of Capri.

"Under way in *La Conchita,* a small but sumptuous vessel, the others went below, but Earnshaw was buttonholed by Brand, who expatiated shrewdly on their fellow guests. The Marchesa Ginori was, of course, Liseta's girl friend—if such a phrase were applicable to this representative of one of the oldest Roman families.

Her husband, the Marchese, was vaguely somewhere. And meanwhile, Liseta was tangibly devoted to her, as the lady's pearls—not an heirloom—seemed to indicate. Earnshaw merely nodded without comment. He had already taken the measure of the elegant Marchesa.

As for Masters, young Charley Masters, went on the colonel, he was a good kid, a writer. A bit shy and raw, maybe, but well on the road to success. He had, in a quiet way, had a big hand in the story end of *Don Alvarez* and was working on a script for Liseta's next film right now.

Inevitably this turned the conversation on their host. Earnshaw, of course, knew of Liseta's staggering success in *Don Alvarez*. Who did not? It was front-page news in half a dozen continents. Liseta, an obscure operatic singer struggling along in mediocrity, had been given his chance by the M.L.M. Corporation in a second-line production, a romantic confection centered round the early Spanish settlers in New Orleans.

No one had much hopes of the film till it was released. And then, in a word, the thing went mad. It blazed to success across the States, in England, France, Germany, Italy and Japan. Liseta's singing, dancing and dashing handsomeness became the topic of the hour. He was written up, publicized, established. A million of his photographs went into circulation and stood in the bedrooms of duchesses and slaveys. And a million phonographs ground out "Light of My Heart," the theme song of *Don Alvarez*.

And then, while the yacht slackened speed and began to sidle into the tiny exquisite harbor, Liseta came on deck with the rest of the party. He struck a theatrical attitude.

"There she is! Beloved Capri—home of Emperors and Félix Liseta."

The words were uttered with colossal satisfaction.

They drove off in two cars, winding up the white road which circled the green mountainside. They climbed and climbed, until at last they reached the heights of Anacapri, where Liseta's villa stood. It was the Villa Paradiso, a lovely spot, the gardens designed with formal charm, the view a breathless panorama of surf-frilled coast which lay, as if in miniature, a thousand feet beneath.

"It is the finest villa on the island. I ought to know. I have just paid for it," remarked Liseta, as he ushered his guests through the patio. His handsome face wore a self-satisfied smirk.

The Earnshaws had two rooms on the west front. As it was already late and dinner was at eight, they changed at once and went down to the studio, a large room on the ground floor with a satinwood grand piano. Everyone was there but Liseta,

At five minutes past eight he came in leisurely, wearing an immaculate dinner suit of fine white material, savoring their appreciation like an epicure. His hair gleamed with a perfect luster; his skin was smooth as a woman's; his nails, freshly pointed, shone with varnish. On the little finger of his left hand was a large Brazilian topaz which exactly matched his eyes. A faint odor of perfume preceded him.

The dinner was excellent and there was a great deal of the best champagne.

"I never drink anything but champagne," explained Liseta. "After all, why not? It is just possible I can afford it! And besides, it pleases my film fans to think of me drinking champagne."

"Incidentally, you must have a terrific fan mail, Félix," suggested the colonel.

Liseta nodded gravely. "Thirty thousand letters every week. My secretary has trunkloads of them."

"You mean you carry them about with you?"

"Why not?" Liseta gazed at Earnshaw, who had asked the question, with serious eyes. "I am very sympathetic, like all great artists. And very sensitive. These letters help me. They come from women all over the world."

" 'Wealth and fame attract women,' " quoted Earnshaw humorously. "An old Chinese proverb."

A slight frown darkened Liseta's brow. He had no sense of humor. He drew himself up with offended dignity.

"You are wrong, Signore. My money and my fame make no difference. Women have always loved me for myself alone."

That night when they went upstairs Rankin turned to his wife with a wry smile. "What a conceited fop the fellow is."

"Oh!"

"Don't you think so?"

"On the contrary, I think he's charming."

His eyes twinkled. "My dear, you think he's charming because he made eyes at you all evening."

She flushed. "Don't be ridiculous. Jealousy doesn't become you. Just because the man happens to be so divinely handsome!"

He watched her, puzzled, yet mildly amused, as she went into her room, closing the door behind her.

Next morning was gloriously fine, a delicious June day alive with light and fragrant airs. Earnshaw came down late after an excellent night's rest to find that Katrine had gone bathing with Liseta. As he remembered her behavior on the previous evening, a momentary concern took hold of him. But it passed quickly.

Many times during the past four years men had lost their heads over Katrine. But Katrine had never lost hers. Before he had married her, people had tried to tell him that Katrine was a willful, selfish child. Yet he had not found her so. Their comradeship had been ideal.

THE TWO swimmers returned about noon in the highest spirits, bursting, in a spate of gaiety and laughter, into the patio where Earnshaw was attempting to occupy himself with a dull novel. There was about them both an extraordinary freshness, such a common bond of youth and beauty that Earnshaw felt suddenly and depressingly paternal. It was absurd; he was only thirty-six, yet it caused a constriction of his heart. He forced a smile.

"Had a good time?"

"Oh, marvelous, Rankin!" Katrine's eyes were shining. "The sea was wonderful—all warm and phosphorescent. We swam in a little cove near the Blue Grotto. We could have stayed in for hours And you ought to have seen Félix dive!"

So it was Félix now. Earnshaw managed to keep his smile going. "He's pretty good, is he?"

Liseta gave a satisfied laugh. "Good? You ought to see, my friend; I cut the water like a knife. As for swimming, I am a fish. If I were not the finest tenor in the world, I would have made myself a champion."

He threw out his chest and, perching on the edge of one of the little metal tables in the courtyard, he draped his gorgeous pink-and-yellow bathrobe about him, then lighted a cigaret. It was a perfect pose, so typically flamboyant it touched the artist in Earnshaw and caused him to forget his vexation.

"You know," he declared suddenly, "I'd like to paint you like that, Liseta."

Katrine clapped her hands. "Oh, do, Rankin. Just look, with the sun there, it would make the loveliest picture. The colors of that robe are magnificent."

"Go ahead, my friend." With a flourish, Liseta took a long, complacent inhalation of his cigaret. "It is not everyone whom Félix Liseta would allow to paint him. But I like you. To oblige you, I give you permission. Only, remember, I cannot have long sittings. I must consider my temperament. I cannot remain still for any length of time."

The patronizing affability took Earnshaw's breath away. He rose silently and fetched a canvas from the house, then with broad slow strokes began the outlines of the portrait.

Liseta, for all his assumption of temperament, sat

like a peacock sunning itself on a wall until the luncheon gong sounded. Then, with a side-glance at Katrine, he declared:

"Enough for today, my friend. I shall sit tomorrow after I swim with your most charming wife."

On the following day Katrine and Félix went to the cove again. It was, so to speak, a logical prelude to the sitting. They went the day after and the next. Earnshaw, though not exactly pleased, did not take these excursions seriously. But about eleven o'clock on the forenoon of Wednesday, as he was fitting up his easel in the patio, the Marchesa Ginori approached him. For a minute she stood sullenly inspecting the blocked outlines of his work.

Though he did not glance up, he sensed her mood which, during the previous evening, had been so hostile to Liseta as almost to create a scene. Now she turned abruptly. She spoke English badly and with a husky intonation.

"Why do you let him make love to your wife?"

Earnshaw took up his palette and began squeezing little snakes of color from his paint tubes. "I presume you would prefer to have him make love to you."

"He was," she burst out, "until you came."

Earnshaw was silent. But she was too angry and overwrought to stop.

"He's no good at all, no good at all. He makes love to any woman. It is his conceit; he is eaten up with vanity. You know who he is, eh? Nobody at all. He pretends he is of a good family. It is all lies. He is only half Italian. Liseta, it is a stage name. Tell your wife. It will please her to know. His mother was a peasant woman from Salerno, and his father performed with a circus. Amusing, eh? And this, the great movie hero, is the result."

"I'm sorry," Earnshaw said stiffly. "I think I understand how you feel. But you're mistaken. I know my wife. She's not likely to fall for a man like Liseta,"

"You're a fool! A wooden English fool!" And with an exclamation of furious impatience the Marchesa flung away.

It was not the most auspicious preface to the next sitting for the portrait. Liseta and Katrine returned from the beach almost immediately, and as Liseta took the spotlight in his exotic robe while Katrine lay watching lazily from a long chair, Earnshaw was conscious of bitter gnawings of suspicion in his breast.

When the gong sounded, Liseta leaped down and advanced toward the wet canvas, which he studied condescendingly.

"Already it begins to look a little like me." He flung an arm round Earnshaw's shoulder in showy friendliness. "You cannot achieve perfection straightway. You must take your time, my friend."

"I'm a slow worker," muttered Earnshaw. "Paint isn't really my medium. I'm an etcher. But you needn't give me more than a couple of further sittings. I can finish it from memory when we've gone."

"But my very dear friend," expostulated Liseta, "it is ridiculous. You must stay longer. It is understood.

Already I have invited Madame to remain."

"It's extremely good of you." Earnshaw fought to control himself. "We must leave you, though, at the end of the week."

"But why?" It was Katrine this time, both plaintive and incredulous.

Speechless, Earnshaw looked from one to the other. He felt mortified, trapped and half betrayed.

For the remainder of the week Earnshaw nursed his smoldering anger and suspicion. He had few words and was conscious that he used them clumsily. This, and a certain dogged perversity, made him refrain from bringing the matter to a head with Katrine.

Besides, he was in love with his wife and the last thing he wished was to make a crude blunder which might upset their happy comradeship. He tried to tell himself that Katrine was neither a fool nor a wanton. This was a mere frivolity which would pass.

Yet during the next two days he was far from reassured. Insensibly, he began to feel a subtle change in the attitude of other members of the party toward him. The colonel was a trifle more loquacious and it seemed to Earnshaw that his eyes were sly and secretly amused. Charley Masters, too, showed signs of unmistakable concern. Charley was transparently a good sort, a long, redheaded, freckled youngster, with intelligent eyes and a sensible and sympathetic mind.

On Thursday evening after dinner he joined Earnshaw in the patio, dropping into an adjoining chair.

The four which Brand had suggested at bridge had fallen through, for the Marchesa had gone upstairs with a headache and Liseta, quite obviously, had been eager to dance. Even now the soft strains of a transmitted tango drifted through the open windows of the studio into the warm night air.

"You don't dance?" Masters asked with apparent idleness.

"Not in the presence of an expert," Earnshaw answered with some bitterness. "It embarrasses me."

"Sure; Liseta's an expert, all right."

"He is at most things, apparently."

A short silence. Masters contemplated the glowing end of his cigaret ruefully.

"It's a fact. Liseta can hit the top all round. He's an athlete. Crack shot; swell fencer; like a fish in the water. You ought to see him sit a horse. He's got real guts, too. Once in the old Melvin-Goodson days he knocked out Joe Calman, who was champ of Oklahoma at the time; for calling him a dago."

"Unfortunately, I am on the side of Joe Calman," returned Earnshaw in a chilled voice. "I find Liseta intolerable. In ten years' time when he runs to seed he'll take to corsets."

"Yeah," sighed Masters. "I guess you're right."

The music changed its tempo here and the eyes of the two men, drawn instinctively toward the open window, fell upon the figures of Liseta and Katrine dancing together. They moved slowly, rhythmically and close to each other.

Félix was an exquisite dancer. There was grace, an infinite lightness, which yet suggested immense vitality, in every step he took. Something insinuating and swaggering, an irresistible force, that was both glamorous and barbaric.

When the figures drifted out of the square of light there was a long silence. Then Charley, leaning forward in the darkness, placed his hand on Earnshaw's knee. He was really moved.

"I like you, Earnshaw. And Katrine's a great kid. You take her away tomorrow. Presto."

"Why don't you suggest that I beat I her?" Rankin paused. "If you write novels you ought to know more about life than that. Coercion's no use with a woman like Katrine."

Another pause. Then there came a loud pealing of the bell at the front door of the villa. Neither paid much attention to the sound, but a moment later they heard Liseta call to them from the studio window. In his hand he held a cable, which he waved with indescribable elation. His voice was exultant.

"I've just had news, my friends. Great news at last. Come quickly, quickly. I must tell you all at once."

In his excitement he made a great stir. Masters and Rankin got up and went toward him. Brand was already in the lounge, standing with Katrine.

Liseta drew himself to his full height. He smiled. "My friends," he said, in a gloating voice. "It is only right I should give you the opportunity to congratulate me. Listen if you please to what they think of Félix Liseta."

Slowly, savoring every word between his rather full lips, he read the cable which had just arrived. A request that he sing during the coming season at the Metropolitan Opera House, New York.

It was the classic pinnacle at last. But even so, there was something odious in his open elation. Earnshaw glanced sideways at his wife. She was gazing at Liseta, her face radiant with delight.

"I have made them acknowledge me. They cannot ignore my genius any longer. I will have them all at my feet when I go to New York. And now, my friends, I am going to do something for you." He looked tenderly at Katrine. "I will sing for you."

His gesture was worthy of an emperor conferring the highest accolade; for he was a jealous guardian of his golden voice, and made it a fixed rule never to sing before a private audience. Now, however, he sat down at the piano and, with an air of careless virtuosity, struck into the opening bars of Schubert's "Frühlingsglaube." A moment later he threw back his head and began to sing.

His voice was magnificent, a pure, clear tenor. Neither the range nor the volume was extreme, but the quality of tone was extraordinarily colored and rich. When Earnshaw shut his eyes he could not repress a thrill of genuine appreciation. When he opened them, he could have struck the singer dead.

For now he had no doubt of Katrine's infatuation. Spellbound, she listened, watching Liseta as he swayed on the piano stool, caressing her with his melting voice.

When the song came to an end he held up his hand in the familiar operatic style. "Please! Do not applaud. I know I have sung divinely. There is no need for you to tell me. When I am happy, I always sing my best. And now for something really to touch the heart."

He began the theme song of his picture *Light of My Heart,* and again as the liquid notes trembled upon the air, he played the troubadour to Katrine. If it had not been so monstrous, Earnshaw would have found it quite fantastic. He was afraid to look at Katrine. The sight of her face—eager and absorbed, her eyes alight, lips slightly parted drinking in the words which dripped with sickly sentiment, so wholly bound to Liseta and his tawdry song—froze the very marrow of his bones.

Abruptly he turned and left the studio. In his room, he left the door half open. He must settle this with Katrine once and for all.

It was late before she came upstairs. She stood in his doorway, detached, hardly seeing him, as though still dazzled by a persistent radiance. She said absently: "I thought you had gone to bed."

"No."

"What's the matter?"

"Don't you know?"

She flushed slowly, but without shame. He had never seen her look more beautiful. Strangely, that infuriated him.

He said brutally: "I'm a little tired of your vulgar intrigue with that clown downstairs."

Her color deepened. "Clown?"

"Yes, clown. A conceited mountebank who dances like a gigolo and reeks of scent."

"How dare you speak of him like that!"

He saw her hands clench fiercely. And now she was pale. Because he knew the symptoms of her anger, he tried a last appeal to reason.

"Katrine! Can't you see him as he really is? For God's sake, throw off this horrible fascination he's put on you."

"Why should I?"

Her answer so staggered him he went as pale as she. He stared at her.

"You're in love with him? Very well, then. I see I must save you from yourself. We leave here tomorrow by the first boat."

She did not answer. For a moment she gazed at him, then almost sadly she turned away. He heard the lock turn as she closed her door.

He slept badly—a night disturbed by uneasy sounds and visions. But when he awoke, he was more determined than ever. He jumped up and, dressing hurriedly, told the servant who brought his coffee to awaken Madame, as they were leaving immediately. A moment later, gulping his coffee moodily by the window, his eye was caught by a small white yacht steaming rapidly across the gulf. It was *La Conchita*.

He gave a low cry and rushed into Katrine's room. She was not there. In a flash he saw that her things were gone. He ran downstairs. No sign of her. But on the bare table of the studio lay a letter in her handwriting addressed to him. He tore it open.

She had left him. She was going with Liseta to New York. She was rapturously in love. She asked for her freedom so that she and Félix might be married.

Earnshaw sank into a chair and buried his face in his hands. He could not believe it, and yet he knew it was true. The idea of pursuit flashed across his mind, then left him. Katrine was blinded by glamour. Nothing would shake her from this mad infatuation, Nothing.

Here Earnshaw raised his head and found himself staring at the unfinished portrait of Liseta which stood on its easel in the corner of the studio. His eyes were dull with pain as they viewed the square of canvas. But suddenly they cleared, filled with an inspiration, a miraculous new hope. Earnshaw rose slowly and went over to the portrait . . .

WHEN THE package arrived, it was a cold and sleety November morning in New York, though all the bad weather in the world could not have dimmed the steady glow of Katrine's happiness. Freed by the swift efficacy of Reno, where Rankin, still absent in Europe, had raised no hindrance, she was safely married to Félix and established in a new apartment overlooking Central Park.

Here she had moved her own things and, entranced by her new existence, yet not unpleasantly reminded of the old, she had created a background worthy of them both. Félix was fulfilling his season at the Metropolitan with unprecedented success. Never before had life held for Katrine such interest, richness and joy,

She sang out from the breakfast room: "It's a most exciting parcel. All sacking and untidy rope. Addressed to us both. Hurry, darling; we'll open it together."

Félix came quickly, already groomed to a hair and immaculate in a blue suit carrying a prominent stripe, patent leather shoes with spats and a large black opal in his tie.

"My sweet." He kissed her tenderly, his manicured hands fondling her possessively. "You still adore me?"

"Of course, Félix," she laughed softly. "But do let's see what's in this package."

They opened it together, like happy children. Then a gasp of astonishment came from Katrine's lips.

"Good gracious!" And then, "Isn't it lovely?"

Félix's eyes flooded with delighted vanity. "I had forgotten all about it. But of course I gave him the commission. It's marvelous, simply marvelous."

It was his portrait, completed at last, sent on by Earnshaw. And it was a masterly piece of work, bold and decisive in line, really striking in its coloring. It was Liseta to the life—easy and assured, brilliantly good-looking, glamorously clad in the glorious bathrobe of pink and yellow. In an access of delight he turned and embraced Katrine.

"You like it, my sweet?"

"I love it, Félix. It's so handsome—so like you."

He purred with pleasure, looking round the apartment until with a sudden grin he nodded toward a vacant space upon the wall. "There! We'll hang it there. The only place for it."

"Oh, but really, Félix—" Katrine smiled indulgently, yet perhaps a little doubtfully, for the place was above the bronze head of Earnshaw. Nothing would do, however, but Félix must have his way. He hung the picture himself.

"Very appropriate, my sweet." he smiled, as he took a tender good-by. "It is your little collection of husbands, eh? Now you will be able to see which you prefer."

She laughed, of course, as she surrendered to his thrilling kiss—Félix's high spirits were so infectious. And all that day she was happy, glancing at the picture from time to time with fond and happy eyes. So eager was she to display the new treasure, she rang up Grace Woolley and invited her for tea.

Grace Woolley was her oldest friend, a small but decided brunette with a sprightly manner, heaps of social thrust, and a husband who sold bonds successfully on Wall Street.

When Grace arrived they embraced enthusiastically; then the visitor skipped toward the fire.

"Now, where is it? Show me quick."

"It's over there, Grace," indicated Katrine with shy pride.

Grace Woolley turned and looked at the picture. For a minute she stared, and then she laughed uncontrollably.

"Why," Katrine gasped incredulously, "what's the matter? Don't you like it?"

Grace Woolley had recovered herself quickly. "It's wonderful—quite a wonderful splash of color."

"Then, why . . ."

There was a strained silence, Grace looked at Katrine, then looked away, forced to explain herself, to answer.

"Well, my dear, there's something about—oh, I don't know. Don't you think it's perhaps—a little blatant?"

Tea was not comfortable after that. Katrine felt a sense of relief when the bell rang and Charley Masters was shown into the room. She had seen a lot of Charley since her marriage to Liseta, and now she welcomed him with extra warmth.

"I'm looking for Félix," he said. "But I suppose he's at the Metropolitan."

"None of your bluff, Charley," said Grace, attempting to recover her vivacity. "It's Katrine you're looking for. We all know you're in love with her."

"No one takes any notice of your nonsense, Grace."

Masters laughed and accepted the cup which Katrine held out to him. Then he caught sight of the portrait. He stood stock-still, gaping at it. Both women watched him intently. At last he said:

"So Rankin's finished the picture, after all."

"Why, yes," answered Katrine, and for some reason she had to force her tone to be casual. "It's his present to Félix and me. Wasn't it good of him?"

"Very," agreed Masters, but his voice was odd and his eyes, avoiding hers, remained fixed on the portrait.

She persisted uneasily: "Don't you think it does Félix justice?"

"Oh, yes," said Masters hurriedly. "It's terribly lifelike," and darting a glance at her, he colored deeply.

When Grace and Masters had gone, Katrine scrutinized the portrait with troubled, loving eyes. What *was* wrong with it? She saw nothing. Nothing but her own dear Félix.

Toward six o'clock, when Liseta came in, he found her stretched upon the low settee, listless and pale. He was on his knees beside her in a second, crying out:

"What's the matter, my sweet?"

Wanly she extended her arms toward him. "Oh, Félix, I'm so glad you're back. My afternoon has been wretched. I've got a raging headache. I'm afraid I can't come with you to the opera tonight."

"Not come?" His face fell; he withdrew slightly. "But what a treat you will miss. It is *Rigoletto*. I am always superb in *Rigoletto*."

She felt too fatigued to answer, and he rose and rang for the light repast he invariably took before the performance. She watched him consume the cup of clear bouillon, the glass of old amontillado, the slice of crisp wheaten toast. How coldly he crunched his toast! With what wounded dignity did he sip the sherry! She saw he was mortally offended with her.

But afterwards, when he had changed and came in to say good-by, his complacency was restored. He tucked a rug round her feet and kissed her significantly.

"Never mind, my sweet. It is your loss if you do not see my *Rigoletto*. And after all, I had almost forgotten. Now you have always my portrait to keep you company."

Katrine told herself it was her nerves, the result of Grace's stupidity and Charley's awkwardness. But as the evening wore on her state became extraordinary. The picture began, apparently, to leer at her; the handsome features wore a look both vulgar and affected. Hanging there above the strong ugliness of Rankin's head, the painting became baroque and simpering, the portrait of a popinjay.

Katrine could stand it no longer. With a cry she jumped up from the couch and stampeded, almost hysterically, into bed.

Next morning, a sharp bright day, Katrine was able to laugh at herself, and all her ridiculous fancies of the night before. She breakfasted early and, tiptoeing past Félix's door so as not to disturb him, went for a long drive. She returned, happy and glowing, about one.

And then, as she entered the apartment, humming,

the portrait met her, greeting her with languishing eyes from the wall. She stopped between alarm and dismay. Her hand flew to her throat. She could have screamed.

Félix came in almost at once, in an admirable humor, full of good news.

"More and more success, my sweet," he declared. "Last night I was *magnifico*. Twelve curtain calls. They would not let me go. And this morning I have word from Hollywood. I must fly there next weekend. One scene of the new picture to be reshot. Well, I will go. But they must pay me treble fees."

She paid no attention to his words, but in a low, intense voice she said: "Félix! I want you to do something for me; I want you to take that picture down."

"What? My portrait!"

"Please, Félix, I haven't asked much of you up to now. I don't like that picture. Let me take it down."

HIS SMOOTH brown skin darkened painfully as the blood rushed into it. "You don't like it, eh? Not good enough for you, perhaps. Let me tell you, I had Arnhem in to see it this morning. You believe him, surely. He says it is a masterpiece. He says Earnshaw never painted anything like it in his life."

"I can't help that, Félix. I don't like the picture. It fills me with misgiving. I hate it. I beg you to take it down."

It was their first quarrel. She felt herself trembling. She caught a look deep in his eyes, oddly reminiscent of the portrait's arrogance. It frightened her. In a panic she flung herself into his arms, sobbing.

"Don't let's fall out about it, Félix. We love each other, don't we, Félix?"

But as she lay against his breast she was acutely conscious of the scent he used.

That night they had a small informal supper party at the apartment—it had been arranged the week before—with Grace Woolley and her husband, Charley Masters, Doctor Theodore from the Metropolitan, and Colonel Brand, at present on one of his periodic homings to New York. Everything passed off with apparent ease. Félix, as usual, talked a great deal, drank a quantity of champagne and enjoyed himself immensely. Katrine smiled brightly at all his sallies. The party broke up rather early, and the Woolleys gave Masters and the colonel a lift to Madison Avenue.

For a minute or two there was silence in the smooth-running limousine; then, deliberately, Woolley said: "What has happened to the turtle doves?"

Grace giggled "It was rather obvious, wasn't it? At least on Katrine's side."

Colonel Brand cleared his throat importantly, with the air of a man who has something to impart. "They say that Earnehaw is a stupid man; at least I've heard him called that. Let me tell you, Earnshaw has just done one of the most devilishly clever things imaginable."

"You mean that picture?" asked Woolley.

"Precisely," said the colonel. "It's a miracle. He's torn the mask off Félix Liseta—he's painted not only the man, but his soul. There it is, naked, on the canvas for Katrine to see."

A silence. Then Masters muttered:

"Poor Katrine! When I looked at that picture tonight, and the bronze, and Katrine . . . She was like a child caught between beauty and the beast."

"Katrine can take care of herself," said Grace Woolley tartly. "It's absurd the way everyone thinks of her in terms of sugar candy. She's a full-grown woman with a mind of her own. She doesn't need your sympathy."

But Charley Masters thought otherwise. He called on Saturday evening at the Liseta apartment. He found Katrine alone, wearing a simple white frock which increased her air of fragile desolation, gazing like one bewitched at the portrait and the bronze which stood beneath it.

"You're such a comfort, Charley." She smiled palely. "I was feeling quite lost when you arrived."

"You didn't go with Félix, after all."

"No. I can't stand the rush. I hate Hollywood, and flying upsets me. Besides, I wanted to be by myself for a bit—to think."

He nodded sympathetically.

"You see, Charley," she murmured, "I'm beginning to wonder if I haven't treated Rankin shabbily. He was such a decent sort. Félix swept me off my feet, you see. And now . . . Oh, well, Charley, it's all pretty hard on me."

Sunday passed with dreary slowness. Katrine felt herself on the verge of a complete breakdown. What she had told Masters was true—she had allowed Félix to go away so that she might have breathing space to free him from that hateful image which the portrait had created in her mind. Now she did not disguise from herself the fact that the portrait had become a nightmare in her life. It was odious, repulsive, horrible.

A terrible temptation seized her to take a knife and slash the canvas into ribbons. But she controlled herself, forced herself to be logical. The portrait was not Félix. It could not be. Félix was her perfect lover and she would see him, her own beloved, with clear eyes, when he came back.

Monday came, and with it the hour of his return. Katrine's agitation was pitiful. When she heard his quick step outside, the blood rushed from her face. Then she felt her heart stand still as the door opened and he came swaggering in, arms theatrically extended, lips wearing their slight smile, his eyes glittering at her.

A faint cry broke from her lips. She saw now with irrevocable clarity. He was exactly the same as the portrait. A wave of horror and repulsion swept over her. When he took her in his arms she almost fainted.

Four days later, Grace Woolley ran into Brand's home on Madison Avenue and asked breathlessly to see him. She was shown to his study.

"Colonel!" she gasped. "It's just happened. Katrine has run off."

He rose slowly, with his usual jaded smile. "My dear lady," he chuckled, "why all this excitement? Whatever you may say, my dear Grace, Katrine is essentially a good woman. Right from the start I staked my oath she'd go back to Earnshaw.

THE ONE CHANCE

I had not seen Dr. Squirnes since before the war, and last winter, when I met him again, I was astounded at the change in him.

Frederick Bamford Squirnes was the leading doctor of Dymchester. Indeed, he was the only doctor of that small, conservative Wessex country town, since no opposition stood up to him for long, and although a stray practitioner might occasionally drift in and put up his shingle, he never did anything against the established physician and, after a few months, invariably drifted out again.

You see, Dr. Squirnes had all the advantages. He came of good-class Dymchester people. Educated at Winchester and Cambridge, he had married into a leading Wessex family—his wife was Lord Sedgefield's second daughter—which gave him the entree, socially and professionally, to the great houses of the district. He rode to hounds, shot over the best coverts, sat as Justice of the Peace on the Dymchester bench, lived in style, in his big red brick Georgian house facing the Square, with a boy in buttons to deliver the medicines, and that indispensable old retainer, Banks, to drive his shining but discreet Rolls-Royce.

When I knew him he was in his prime, not yet fifty, and he had been a widower for three years. His figure was erect and military, his jaw square, his eyes blue, his complexion ruddy from his outdoor life and the vintage port he drank after dinner. Immaculately turned out, he curled his short mustache in cavalry style, and looked like a colonel of hussars.

Indeed, his unchallenged position, added to a proud and choleric disposition, had made of him a thorough autocrat. In his own phrase, "he stood no nonsense from his patients." Even with the surrounding gentry his word was law. As for the local tradespeople and farmers, they often trembled in his presence. For he had a way of damning a man for knocking him up late, or for not knocking him up at all, which fell little short of bullying.

Despite his stiff-necked arrogance, his reputation as a doctor stood high. His methods, which were honest and forceful, suited the rustic mentality. He believed in a few fundamental remedies—senega and sulphur, nux vomica, fresh air, and good mustard plaster. He could purge and poultice, set a bone well, starve a fever and reduce an inflammation. Experience had given him a rare "nose" for a dangerous disease—he could scent it the moment he entered a sickroom.

Nothing pleased him better than to hear himself referred to as a "sound" man. Yes, a sound man, who had no truck with any newfangled rubbish—those catchpenny vitamins and vaccines which were here today and gone tomorrow. If any man had dared to hint that he was old-fashioned, he would have pointed to his results, to his magnificent practice, and told him—I have no doubt—to go to the devil.

DR. SQUIRNES had one child, a daughter named Elizabeth who, when she was twenty-one, married the son of a London solicitor. The match was not exactly to Squirnes' taste—he would have preferred for his daughter someone drawn from the Dymchester aristocracy. However, the young man was not long destined to incur his father-in-law's displeasure. Within five years the war broke out, and, called up as a reserve officer, he was killed at Dunkirk.

Immediately Dr. Squirnes invited Elizabeth and her little girl, Mary, to make their home with him. It seemed a perfect arrangement—he was extremely attached to his four-year-old granddaughter and could offer her every advantage. Elizabeth, however, although quiet and reserved, had a mind of her own and did not always see eye to eye with her imperious father. She held out for a separate home and gained her point by renting "Gable-ends," a pleasant Tudor cottage opening on the Dymchester Green quite near the doctor's house.

Here began a great new interest for Dr. Squirnes. The war years were increasing his work, making him more arbitrary and irascible, yet there was rarely a day when he did not find half an hour to spend with the fair-haired, blue-eyed child at "Gable-ends." Like most martinets, he had a hidden strain of sentiment. He loaded Mary with attentions, put a pony in the paddock for her, took her driving with him on Sunday if the weather was fine. He was delighted when Lady Sedgefield remarked that the little girl "favored him" in many ways.

ONE DAY an event occurred in Dymchester which at first sight seemed to warrant less than a passing interest—a new doctor arrived and opened a surgery in the High Street. Yet perhaps there was some novelty in the fact that the newcomer was a woman—not only a woman, but a foreigner, an Austrian refugee from Vienna.

Squirnes first heard the news from Banks, who detailed it to his master, with an ironic slant to his well-drilled features, concluding:

"Judgin' by the others, sir, I gives her a month."

Dr. Squirnes, preoccupied with a long visiting list in the back of the car, grunted a reply. He had barely heard. But on the following Sunday afternoon when a young woman called upon him at his house, introduced herself as Dr. Frieda Hahn, and explained that she was making a "visit of etiquette," he did recollect his man's remark, and the blood rose to his forehead. Etiquette, indeed! Did this confounded alien presume to speak to him of manners! He had always hated the idea of women in medicine; they had neither the head nor the hands for it. Besides, she had interrupted his sacred after-luncheon nap. If she had even been pretty it might have constituted an extenuating circumstance, but she was quite plain, with a pale face, dark hair and bespectacled greenish-brown eyes. And oh, how dowdily she was dressed—in a cheap black skirt and dark gray blouse. Freezingly, he advised her that he was engaged, then rang for her to be shown out.

She rose as the servant appeared. "I'm sorry if I've disturbed you, Doctor. But I hope we shall cooperate in our work."

He gazed down at her in his best Chesterfieldian manner. "In what work, pray, madam?"

"Why"—she looked surprised—"in our practices."

"Madam," he answered cuttingly, "in Dymchester there is only one practice."

She studied him with a kind of vague wonder, scarcely comprehending. The door closed upon her.

For several weeks Dr. Squirnes heard nothing of the intruder. Yet, in some queer way, although she was so far beneath his notice, he kept alert for news of her departure, waiting for Banks to remark, between deference and amusement, "We was right about that furriner, sir. She packed and left last night."

Yet when news did reach him, it was of a different nature. Since Dr. Squirnes was held in universal deference, and surrounded by a loyal staff, unpleasant information did not easily filter through to him, yet filter it did, and it all spoke unmistakably, disturbingly, of Dr. Hahn's successes.

Testily, he told himself it was local gossip. Yet there were facts which could not be so easily dismissed. In the case of Farmer Digby's wife, for instance—by prescribing a special diet, Dr. Hahn apparently had cured a painful dermatitis on which Dr. Squirnes had tried his ointments in vain. Then Henry Drake's asthma, those desperate nocturnal attacks of breathlessness which had baffled him for years, seemed to have yielded to some confounded injection which she had used. Again, with an electrical machine, she had cleared up the facial paralysis which had affected young Pratt, the corn chandler's boy, ever since his mastoid operation. This last stung Dr. Squirnes worst of all, for it was his overbold incision that had damaged the nerve, and he had shrugged off the affliction which followed as incurable, an act of God.

His mortification grew, and with it his resentment. Who was this female refugee? By what right did she practice medicine here? Goaded by his anger, he sent a strong telegram to the Secretary of the Medical Association in London querying that right, asking for specific information on Dr. Frieda Hahn.

The answer, which came promptly, dashed his hopes and added to his dismay. Affably and at length, the secretary explained that Dr. Hahn was a gifted young Viennese physician, who not only had several Continental degrees, but had, on her arrival in England, taken the London M.D. with honors.

Dr. Squirnes tore up the telegram into small pieces, his face grim. Then he squared his shoulders, reflecting on his assured position, his fine house, his innumerable advantages. His lip curled. Let this brilliant lady have her brief moment with his "castoffs," who were always ready to flock to anyone new. She would come a cropper soon enough.

But the months slipped past and Dr. Hahn gave no sign whatsoever of coming to grief. On the contrary, she went on, calmly and unobtrusively, cutting into the very roots of Squirnes' practice. Her scientific technique and her modest yet masterly methods were now on everyone's lips. She was unassuming, too, and extremely gentle. Almost with a start the townspeople realized how long they had put up with "the old doctor's high-handed ways." And so, alas, did many of the gentry. Outside those mansions where the shining and discreet Rolls-Royce had once proudly stood, there now was seen, somewhat chipped yet jauntily propped, a black-enameled bicycle.

For Frederick Bamford Squirnes this humiliation, steady and progressive, became the bitterest anguish. He fancied that people were talking of him behind his back. In the streets he saw commiseration in every glance, found in the simplest greeting an undertone of pity. Even his servants seemed uneasy, afraid to meet his eye. At night, brooding in his study, he told himself he would have welcomed competition from an equal, say some bustling youngster from his own university; but to be eclipsed by this outsider was something he could not, would not endure. Words rose to his lips which were unutterable. Hating her with a new intensity, he gritted his teeth and swore he would get the better of her.

ONE AFTERNOON in late November he returned from his round to find that a call had come in for "Gable-ends"—his daughter had rung up to say that Mary had a headache and was slightly indisposed. Amidst many desertions and discouragements, this loyalty cheered Squirnes—at least he stood first with his own family. He told himself he would go round when he had drunk a cup of tea. But on his way to his study the telephone drew him up. It was Elizabeth again, asking him with a note of urgency to come at once. Mary had been taken with something of a fit.

Dr. Squirnes was at the cottage within four minutes. Elizabeth looked scared as she met him at the door and led him upstairs to the nursery. And the moment his eyes fell upon the convulsed child, lying semiconscious amidst her scattered toys, his own heart contracted with a sudden fear. His instinct and experience told him the condition was serious.

Acting quickly, he relieved the immediate symptoms, then made a careful examination. When he had finished, his face was unnaturally pale. But, summoning all his resources, his powers of dissimulation, he reassured the anxious mother, wrote out several prescriptions, promised to return without fail later that evening. He came back in an hour, once again before midnight, and twice the next morning. Also, he brought in his old friend, the matron of the town hospital, to act as nurse, with the head sister of his own ward to aid her.

BY THIS TIME there was no concealing the gravity of the case from Elizabeth. Distraught, she pressed her hands together, begged him for the truth. He had to tell her—it was the most painful duty of his life. Mary had cerebrospinal meningitis.

She stared at him, not quite comprehending, and murmured with trembling lips, "We must do something."

"We're doing everything... everything...." He put his arm round her shoulders, striving to control his own emotion. "You know I love her, too."

All that day Mary grew worse. She was not especially robust, and the virulence of the infection was acute. Already her face had shrunk to nothing, and her forehead, crowned by an ice bag, seemed to bulge above her squinting eyes. The convulsions had exhausted her. Throughout the night, Dr. Squirnes remained at the cottage, taking spells of fitful rest on the drawing-room couch. At the breaking of the gray and troubled November dawn he faced Elizabeth across the child's bed. In a low and broken voice he told her there was no hope.

He had expected an outburst of sobs, but instead, Elizabeth was silent; then, with a set face, she lifted her eyes toward him.

"Father," she said. "I want Dr. Hahn to see Mary!"

It was as though a dagger had entered his heart. He gazed at his daughter, almost imploringly.

"No, Elizabeth," he pleaded. "It is quite useless."

"I want Dr. Hahn," she repeated.

"But, my dear," he groaned. "You know my position . . . if you, my own daughter, call that woman in . . . and all to no purpose . . ."

For the third time she said, "I want Dr. Hahn."

He bowed his head. His shoulders were bent as he turned and went downstairs. Only his love for Mary prevented him from leaving the house. He went into the breakfast-room and sank into a chair.

Presently he heard the front door open. It was she. He waited, stubbornly resolved not to consult with her, listening to the voices, the movements on the floor above. Then, after a pause, Dr. Hahn entered the room and stood before him.

HE GOT TO his feet, strung to breaking-point, yet making himself look at this hated woman, aware that for the sake of Elizabeth and the child, for his own sake, he must maintain a fitting dignity. He listened rigidly as she began to speak, expressing her sympathy, holding herself in complete agreement with his diagnosis. Despite the torment in his heart, a pale glow pervaded him at this sign of her approval.

There was a silence. Then she said, "I think there is just one chance." He started, but before he could reply, she named a specific drug which at that time was quite unknown.

Penicillin. He simply did not know what she meant. Was it one of these newfangled remedies, those worthless innovations which came and went like waves upon the shore? He had never heard of it. He gazed at her, completely at a loss, as, hurriedly, she described it as a mold, violently destructive to certain germs, and as yet barely past the experimental stage. But its originator, only last month, had used it with success upon a patient suffering from the same disease that had stricken Mary. Although it was not yet upon the market, she believed she could obtain a supply of the new drug within four hours. Had she his permission to use it—if it were not too late?

Torn by opposite emotions, he made a blind gesture which must have passed for acquiescence. She left him immediately and hurried to the telephone in the hall.

Dully, he climbed the stairs to the sickroom and stood at the foot of the bed. Dear God, he could see that it was nearly over. The child lay, almost lifeless, in the coma preceding dissolution.

A terrible sense of the futility of Dr. Hahn's action suffocated him. To what purpose had she raised false hopes in the poor mother's breast? Did he not know death? Had he not seen it, grim and implacable, a hundred times before? Only a charlatan would have dared to desecrate this final, solemn hour.

All his feeling for the child supported this frightful mood of bitterness. When, at last, Dr. Hahn appeared with a package, his face was gray and frozen, except for the twitching of his cheek. Motionless, he watched while she prepared the drug for injection. As the needle entered the pulseless body, he would have sworn that the end had come. A culminating tide of anger and despair surged over him. Lacerated, outraged, he could bear it no longer. He turned and broke from the room.

Straight ahead he walked, out of the house, and toward the open country, bareheaded, his hands clenched, heeding no one. He must have tramped many miles, across the fields, through hedges and ditches, spattering himself with mud, tearing his clothing upon the briars. It was very late when he got home. Exhausted, he went straight to his room, flung himself upon his bed. He slept at once and heavily, as though he had been stunned.

Next morning, it was past nine when he awoke. The maid who brought his tea gave him a frightened glance. She told him that Elizabeth had telephoned him twice. Well, they would wish him to make arrangements for the funeral. Afterward—his lips drew to a thin line—he would have his interview with Dr. Hahn.

He rose, dressed with his accustomed care, went out. Then, as he descended his front door steps, he saw his daughter hurrying up the street. She ran toward him, radiant.

"Father," she cried. "Mary is better."

Stupefied, he searched her face, thinking that she had gone out of her mind.

"Yes," Elizabeth nodded joyfully. "She is conscious. And her temperature has fallen four degrees."

"What!" The exclamation came from him mechanically.

"It's true, Father. Dr. Hahn says she is out of danger."

Without a word he turned and accompanied her down the street. He did not believe her. The child had been moribund when he left the room. No power on earth could have saved her.

He was breathing heavily as be entered the nursery. And there, on the threshold, he drew up, transfixed. Mary, limp but fully conscious, was drinking some bouillon which the matron held to her lips. One hand clasped her favorite rag doll. The other she extended feebly toward him, in recognition.

A sob broke from Dr. Squirnes. Something within him snapped and crumpled, as though the whole structure of his personality, the very foundations of his soul, were falling into ruins. He raised his hand to his head. Dizzily, he knelt down beside the cot, unmindful of the tears streaming from his eyes.

THE DAYS and weeks which followed were strange indeed for Frederick Bamford Squirnes. Apparently impassive, he went about his work, regardless of the stir created by the case in Dymchester. Yet to himself he was like a man living in a dream. Mary had gone with her mother to Devon for a long convalescence. He felt singularly alone, and in this new solitude, time and again he was taken by an overmastering desire to see Dr. Hahn. But always he resisted it.

Then, one January morning, as he drove out on his round, his man Banks remarked, in a restrained voice, "I hear Dr. Hahn is leaving us, sir."

Squirnes' heart gave a sudden violent bound. He leaned forward. "Why?"

"I don't know, sir." Banks spoke soberly. "But I'm sure we're all real sorry."

Now he could resist no longer. That same day, after dusk, Dr. Squirnes walked to the small house in the High Street where Frieda Hahn lived. She was writing at the table as he entered the small book-lined sitting-room, and her look of surprise made him redden painfully.

"I ought to have come before," he said in a low tone. "To express my profound and heartfelt thanks."

"Ah!" She smiled faintly. "A visit of etiquette."

His color deepened, then faded. Pale but resolute, he said, "I have come for another reason. To ask you not to leave Dymchester."

"Indeed! Wasn't it you who suggested I should depart?"

"All the more reason why I should now beg you to stay."

Her surprise was unmistakable. But quickly, nervously, he went on, "You are needed here. If it should be an inducement to you . . . if you could work with me . . . I came to ask you to join me in partnership."

"Ah! You think it would be advantageous to unite the practices." She could not repress the ironic lift of her brows. "But didn't you say there was only one practice in Dymchester?"

He was quite silent. And, gazing at him closely, she saw how he had altered, how drawn he had become, how the lines had gathered around his eyes.

"I'm sorry." She rose impulsively. "Your offer is kind and generous. But I cannot accept it. I am going—I must go—back to Austria, to a clinic we are opening in Vienna for the children."

"But you'll come back."

She shook her head. "My work is there."

There was a long pause.

"Well." He sighed. "I will say good-by. And once again, thank you."

"Wait." She detained him; took him by the arm. "I think you are right. You could do with a young partner . . . someone whose new ideas would unite with your solid worth. And I could send you such a one . . . a young doctor . . . clever, oh, yes . . . but half-starved, with an incipient tuberculosis. He has been four years in a concentration camp, and we have just got him out, more dead than alive." She paused, looking him directly in the eyes. "But then . . . you would not want him. . . . He is Polish."

His eyes did not falter under her gaze. He smiled.

"You have taught me many things. How little I know of medicine, for instance. But most of all how little I really know of people. When can you send him along?"

DR. SQUIRNES is not now the only doctor in Dymchester. He has a partner—a skinny, dark-eyed young Pole with an unpronounceable name who reads all the medical journals and whose cough is rapidly clearing up in the good Wessex air.

Some people wonder why the old doctor should have chosen such a singular associate. They say he has changed—that his pride has been replaced by oddity. But he is not altogether reformed, thank heavens. He still swears at his patients occasionally, and once in a while he swears at his youthful colleague. But there is a new tolerance in his manner, a gentleness and sympathy which were never there before. He uses his fine Rolls-Royce much less, and even talks of buying himself a bicycle. Every Sunday, in place of his usual nap, he writes a weekly letter to Vienna. Then he walks along, stooping more than he did and smiling to himself, to take tea with Mary and Elizabeth.

They say he is "not the man he was!" People do not look up to him nearly so much. But—and this was never so before—they are beginning to love him.

Lightning Source UK Ltd.
Milton Keynes UK
UKHW020725130520
363166UK00017B/266